Monday

"Hey, how are you doing Men?" asks Officer Long displaying his thick southern drawl. His older, white frail body, sits comfortably behind his freshly polished wooded desk, inside of his newly renovated office.

In front of him stands, Eric Johnson, a tall young slender black man, standing attentively along with his co-worker Jermaine Williams an equally tall, but muscular young black man.

"Great," replies Maine, looking around to all of Officer Long's many accolades neatly planted alongside the walls.

"Fine," follows Eric.

"Well first of all I have to say that I'm truly pleased with the work the two of you have been putting in around here. Coming in early, staying late, not to mention the fact that it seems as if all of the inmates respect you. I mean from the trespassers to the murders, you guys just know how to handle them," he says as he reclines back in his seat. "To be honest, it's rare. Everyone isn't built to work here at the Norfolk City Jail. I've been around for a long, long time. 30 years, next spring. I've seen it all. Everything from the guys who let inmates walk all over them, the wanna be tough guys, the whiners, corrupt ones. Basically, any kinda guy you can imagine. But I've yet to see many like you two," he says as he points to his men. "I've always said that it takes a special breed to successfully handle hundreds of emotionally unstable, caged up men. You've gotta have tough skin to excel in this line of work," he says as Eric and Maine, both nod. "Too be so young you guys are on your way to a very prosperous career. And with that being said. I have a very special task for you," he says as he now sits erect. "Like every summer, the jail population has skyrocketed out of this world. We don't have an inch of space left around here and due to the fact that we can't risk placing 'Arieus Hatch' next to any other inmates. I've came up with a plan," he says as he stands to his feet. "As you all know 'Samuel Pete Turner' has been housed here for the last month awaiting his appeal this Thursday."

"Yeah," they both say in Unison.

"He's already been in Federal Prison for the past 3 years and I'm pretty sure he doesn't want anything to ruin his chances of getting out. Especially considering the fact that he was sentenced to 181 years. Therefore he really has no room for an opinion on who we decide to put in his cell," he says as he walks to the edge of his desk and takes a seat. "As you two may already know we've been hiding him down in the basement cell since his arrival. The Feds wanted to make sure no inmates knew he was in custody. But with his cell being the only free one we have around here, I've decided to throw Arieus down there with him."

"So you're telling us that you're actually gonna put them in the same cell together?" asks Maine, surprised.

"It's the only choice I have. But what I want you two to do," he says as he points over to them both. "Is monitor them for your 12 hour shifts. Simple task, I have a couple other guys who'll patrol them when you guys go home. It'll be gravy, all you'll have to do is sit in the patrol room, watch the camera and feed them. Think of it as like a mini vacation. Give you some time to get your mind off of all the buffoonery going on around here." He finishes as Eric and Maine look over to one another pleasantly nodding. "They both will only be here for another week or so. The hardest thing you guys will have to do is keep Arieus safe. If this Pete character has a problem with what we're doing. Which I'm sure he initially will, then that's his loss," he says, shrugging his shoulders. "I don't know why but I'm really feeling good this week, so I guess I can allow one physical altercation before I reprimand him. I don't think he's that stupid though. With everything going on with him I seriously doubt he's willing to risk it all. But in the case that he does assault Arieus, just take him down to the boiler room for a few hours. We've already got a mat sat up. After burning up down there, I'm sure he'll tighten right on up. You guys got a problem with that?"

"No sir," says Eric.

"Nope not at all," follows Maine.

"Great. Well Arieus is being housed in the Nurses offices. We've been hiding him up there since he's arrived. I'll buzz over and let her know you're on your way up."

2

"Thanks for trusting us with the job sir," says Maine as he and Eric both nod in approval.

"No. Thank you guys for being the kinda workers we can all be proud of," he says with a smile, extending his arm for a handshake.

They both shake hands.

"No problem sir," says Eric.

"That's what we're here for," follows Maine as they exit the office.

The two men step foot from the comforts of Officer Long's office. There is a drastic change in scenery. Gone are the hardwood floors and fluorescent lights. Instead they've been replaced with cracked cemented floors and flickering bulbs that seemed to be on their last leg.

As Eric presses the corroded 'Up' button on the elevator directly across from Officer Long's office, he speaks. "Yo bro, that nigga Pete gonna be mad as hell."

"It's crazy right? How they gonna bunk a supposed 'Cop Killer' with a 'Cop who kills niggas," says Maine.

"Shit, fuck it, aint my business, I'm just here for a check," Eric follows as the elevator door opens and they step inside.

"Nigga, who you telling," says Maine as he presses the number four. "I just hope the nigga Pete don't kill that cop in his sleep or something."

"Dog, Ima be honest. I don't give a fuck what he does. Long as the shit don't effect me."

"You damn sure have a point there my brother," Maine says as they slap hands. "Ay bro you heard that new Korb SKii mixtape?"

"Korb Skii? Man you already know I'm not listening to that bullshit."

"Bullshit?" asks Maine. "Do you even know who Korb Skiii is?"

"Nope," replies Eric. "But there's no way in hell I'm listening to one of these new school skinny jean makeup wearing, mumbling pussy's."

The two exit the elevator onto the empty hallway. Nothing's changed. Still gloomy, only now the complaints of sick or wounded inmates can be heard through the closed steel cell doors as the odor of stale breath plagued, giving off the feeling that simply inhaling too hard could result in dropping dead from some sort of soul snatching disease.

"What? Nigga you young your damn self. You the same age as me, 28. Stop acting like a fuckin Grand Daddy all the time," says Maine as the two make their way to the Nurses office.

"Grand Daddy? Nigga aint nobody acting like a damn Grand Daddy. I just grew up in a time where Rap was real. Pure. A guy had to have some real talent to call himself an MC. It won't all this fuckery going on."

"And niggas nowadays don't have talent?"

"Hell No," bolts Eric. "Nigga are you serious? Is that even a question? Hell, to be honest I have no idea what 80% of these cats are

4

even saying. To keep it real, all I hear is gibberish. I can't lie the beats be sick, but that's fuckin it."

"Man that's cause you're stuck in your ways and all you choose to hear is gibberish, I understand though. I'm not mad at you. I just know that you don't good know music."

"Good Music? Nigga that aint no damn music. How many times I got to hear that you whippin, flippin and finessin a brick," asks Eric in a mocking tone.

"First of all that aint all every rapper talks about. Korb SKii, J.Cole, Kendrick, Big Sean, none of them talk about no fucking bricks. Secondly, obviously it's a big problem in the community if that's what they chose to rap about. Their just a reflection of our reality."

"Man, I aint tryna hear that bullshit. Rappers from 10 years ago had the same reality and they still didn't rap like Gucci Mane."

"Whoa. Are you crazy?" asks Maine before stopping dead in his tracks, placing his hands over his heart in disbelief. "Don't ever speak bad about Gucci. Ever."

"What?" he asks looking back at Maine. "Are you kidding me? You gotta be stupider than I thought to even take someone like him serious. Out of all this new shit. He's by far the worse. Hands down."

"First of all my nigga aint new," says Maine as they continue walking. "He's been in the game more than 10 years. Shit, if it won't for him we wouldn't have Future, Migos, Young Thug, Waka, he even had a hand in Nicki Minaj's career. No question, he's the hardest working man in the industry."

"Like I said, he sucks and if he had any part in bringing any of those clowns in the game than I hate him even more than I thought."

"Nigga, fuck you. I'm done with this convo."

"You need to be done with they weak asses."

"You retarded," says Maine as he knocks on the nurse's door.

Lakenda Martin, a plus sized middle aged black woman opens up. "Hey."

"Whatsup Kenda," says Maine as he and Eric enter.

Eric nods as he looks around the small office. The smell of febreze noticeably offsets the sickening stench from the hallway, allowing both Eric and Maine to finally breathe comfortably.

While the lighting again changes, although not quite as bright as Officer Long's headquarters, it's nowhere near close to being as dull and depressing as the hallway had been.

"Nothin much," she says before whispering.

"Waiting for yall to get this crazy motherfucker out my office," she says pointing over to a white sheet, splitting the room in half.

"Every time I look over there the shit just makes me mad."

They snicker as they slide over to the sheet. Pulling it back, Maine blurts, "Oh shit,"as he discovers Arieus Hatch dressed in an orange jumpsuit, staring blankly at the ceiling.

He slowly turns his head towards them, his eyes seem to be facing all three workers but his eyeballs seem to be lacking something

6

major, similar to a wounded animal. Being deprived of normal sunlight, his skin has grown pale all the way from his face to his visibly exposed shackled up ankles that dangle from his small metal twin sized bed.

"Yo yall keep him locked to the bed all day like this?" asks Eric, looking over to Arieus's right wrist which is cuffed to the bed rail.

"You damn right we do," answers Lakenda. "What other options do he have? It's either this or he can get his ass whipped in general population. Yall must be crazier than him if you think for a second I was going to stay in here all day with him roaming around freely," she says, causing everyone to laugh.

"So he doesn't say a word anytime other inmates come in?" asks Eric.

"Nope. Actually he hasn't said a word the entire time he's been in here. Usually I'd like that but it's been kinda freaking me out," says Lakenda as they all look over, noticing that Arieus is still staring.

"Yall do realize we're talking about him as if he isn't just sitting right over there," adds Maine.

"Boy please. Fuck him. Aint nobody thinking about how he feels. If it was up to me his ass would be doing a damn life sentence instead of 8 days. I damn sure wish I could kill somebody and get away with it. Must be nice," follows Nurse Kenda.

"Hell yeah," says Maine. "And the crazy thing is, I heard he's still eligible to go right back on the Police force when he gets out."

7

"The world we live in," says Kenda, looking over to Arieus, disgusted.

"Crazy," says Maine as he shares, Kenda's disgusted look. "You're right fuck him."

"Yeah get your ass up," demands Eric.

"Nigga you saying that like he not shackled up," follows Maine.

"Oh yeah," Eric says before walking over to Arieus. "Put your left hand next to your shackled hand," he demands before cuffing him up as Arieus scoots from off of the bed, still never making eye contact.

"We moving you downstairs to the basement cell," says Maine as Arieus continues staring blankly. "Ay man," Maine follows as he snaps his fingers in the face of Arieus. "You gotta start talking dog. All this mute shit is in the way."

"Yeah your ass wont retarded when you killed little Bobby," follows Eric.

"8 fucking days," Kenda adds. "Hurry up and get him out of here. I can't take his vibe for one more second."

"Yeah whatever," replies Maine. "We know the real reason you want him to get out. You just can't wait to get freaky with the inmates when they come in. I heard about you," Maine jokes.

"You aint heard shit about me. Aint no way in hell I'd touch anybody in this trifling jail. I go home to something real nice EVERYnight," she says as she puts an enfaces on every.

8

"Yeah, yeah we know you love your vibrator," says Eric, jokingly.

"Get your ass out of here," says Lakenda, laughing as she motions for them to leave.

"See ya later. Have a good day." says Maine, smiling as the three men make their way out of the office.

"Yeah whatever," replies Lakenda as she closes the door behind them.

They stroll back down the gloomy hallway, Arieus in front.

"Ay nigga speed your ass up. Don't nobody care that you got shackles on," barks Eric.

"Yeah, nigga you lucky I don't trip your bitch ass," follows Maine as he and Eric both burst out into laughter as Arieus continues to display his calm demeanor.

"Naw but foreal, nigga speed your ass up. I'm tryna get in that control room and get a sample of my lunch. I'm hungrier than a mo'fucker and Shwanda cooked me a bomb ass meal."

"Shwanda?" I thought you said you was done with that bitch."

"Hold on nigga. Why she gotta be a bitch?" asks Eric, angrily.

"Nigga you just called her a bitch yesterday."

"See that's exactly why your ass aint never gone make it nowhere. Always thinking about the fucking past. Grow up."

"Whatever nigga."

"But if you would like to know, me and Shwanda had a talk."

"About what?"

"Us nigga."

"Eric," Maine says looking over to his partner. "I'm sorry to say this. But you stupid."

"What nigga? You stupid," rebuts Eric.

"Nigga that bitch is using you," shouts Maine as they approach the elevator.

"Bro I aint gon lie," says Eric as he presses the down button. "I love working with you. You may have some dumbass opinions sometimes. But all in all you a good nigga. But if you say one more word about my baby, neither one of us will be working here. I'm gonna be in jail for the rest of my life and your ass gon be dead," speaks Eric as the aging elevator door opens and they step out once again.

"Dead?" questions Maine as he presses the button that reads ground.

"Yeah nigga, Dead," he says, pausing, looking square into Maine's eyes.

"Nigga you crazy, how you gonna get mad when all I'm tryna be is a good friend?"

"Good Friend. Where? All I see is a negative hater. Shwanda warned me about niggas like you."

"Man fu--," shouts Maine before rephrasing his words. "Man forget her. She don't cook."

"Nigga I told you she cooked for me today," Eric interrupts.

"Nigga like I said, she don't cook, don't clean. And not to mention. When the last time you got your dick sucked? Huh?"

10

The elevator door opens and the trio step into the basement. This atmosphere is by far worse than both other floors combined. Along with everything that plagued those hallways, this one happens to be cold, damp and creepishly darker.

Arieus leading the way, they walk straight ahead in a single fine line as drops of water fall onto their heads from the leaky pipes hanging from the low ceiling.

"Why the hell you worried bout my dick?" Eric continues as they head to a closed steel cell about 30 feet in front of them.

"What? You the one who come to work bitching every day."

"No the fuck I don't."

"What? Are you serious? Let me refresh your motherfucking memory. Just last week you came to work complaining cause she didn't come home."

"Yeah but I found out her car broke down and her charger to her phone broke," follows Eric.

"Ok well how about the week before that when she got mad at you for really no damn reason and launched that dresser drawer at you."

"Nigga that shit normal. Love hurt sometimes."

"Bro she damn near gave you a concussion. You had to get 8 stitches in your head."

"So. Nigga, you forgot about when I showed her who's boss and punched her right in her damn face?

"Nigga," Maine shouts. "You proud of that? You lucky she aint call the police. You know you would've gotten fired. Plus, who

11

would've bonded you out? Huh? I got too much child support to be getting you out. And her no job having ass sure aint got no money."

"Man whatever," says Eric huffing and puffing as they continue walking.

"I hope you aint getting upset," adds Maine. "Think about how many times you came to work mad as hell because she don lost another job. How many times yall lights don got cut off? How many times she help you get them back on?" continues Maine as Eric speeds up, pushing Arieus along ignoring Maine. "My nigga. You tried to kill yourself!"

"Man I won't really gon do it," says Eric never looking back.

"Bro. The Dr. had to pump your stomach to keep your ass alive. I'm just saying my nigga. That shit aint worth it. You losing yourself. I remember when you used to fuck every bitch that came across your path with no problem. Who are you?"

"Nigga, I'm me. I just grew up," says Eric finally turning around to look at Maine as the two guard's pause, while Arieus continues to walk. "Maybe you need to do the same. Matter fact, I'm not even gonna speak about her no more. That's my woman dog. She make me feel like no one has ever made me feel before. It's like we got a special connection."

"Nigga that's the gayest shit I ever heard," bolts Maine.

"Fuck you nigga," Arieus spats as he angrily turns around, continuing their path.

The two men walk in silence for the duration of the trip until finally they approach the cell at the very end of the hall where Arieus would be housed.

Whipping out a large set of keys Maine opens the 6x9 cell as Eric removes the shackles from Arieus's feet and cuffs from his wrist. Inside, there is a small bunk bed placed against the wall, where Samuel 'Pete' Turner is fast asleep wearing nothing but his underwear on the bottom bunk.

Across from it sits a small rusty metal sink, attached to a matching toilet, in dire need of a thorough cleaning.

"Nigga go in there," says Eric as he shoves him inside, awakening Pete.

"Yo," Pete screams as his eyes seem to nearly pop out of his head at the site of his new roomy. "What the fuck yall doing? Fuck you putting him in my cell for? Kinda shit yall on?" he screams as he hops out of his rack approaching the officers and Arieus.

"Ay man. We just work here. We don't got nothing to do with this," says Maine with both hands in the air, backing away from the cell as Eric slams it shut.

Arieus slowly walks, unfazed as Pete stands, feet planted forcing him to slightly brush past his shoulder. "Nigga you better watch who the fuck you bumping," Pete blurts. Paying him no mind Arieus proceeds to set up shop, hopping up to the top bunk as Pete angrily looks around confused shaking his head, "I can't believe this shit," he yells.

"Believe it," says Eric. "You're only here for another week or so anyway. Deal with it."

"What?" shouts Pete once again. "Deal with it? It seem like they want me to get into trouble. Yall already know I'ma end up beating his ass. Yall got me caged up with the most hated nigga in the country and yall expect for me to just sit here and not do shit. "

"It's up to you. You wanna fuck up everything you got going on. Be my guest," says Eric.

"Man this shit foul," says Pete, banging his fist against the steel cell as Maine and Eric walk away.

There's an eerie silence as Arieus, lays stiff staring to the ceiling before he soon falls asleep.

During this time, Pete can't seem to find a comfortable spot as he tosses and turns, mumbling to himself for almost an hour before eventually dozing off only to have his slumber quickly snatched from him by Arieus's thunderous scream. "**Ahhhhhhh**."

"Yo what the fuck wrong with you?" screams Pete hopping up from his rack. He, stands tall at 6'1, able to have a clear view of Arieus. Face balled up, he studies him, attempting to discover what the problem was that had interrupted his sleep. As he scanned Arieus's body who was now sitting up, he noticed what looked like urination covering his bottom half. "What the fuck," he screams before the stench hits his nose, letting him know that it was indeed urination that he'd smelt. "You stinky murdering bitch," screams Pete.

Like a deer caught in headlights, Arieus stares speechless causing Pete to grow enraged. "Nigga what the fuck you looking at?" Pete yells.

Continuing to stare, never blinking, Pete loses his cool, hopping to the top bunk, pounding away at Arieus's face and body. With no time to react, Arieus simply covers up, attempting to barricade himself from the blows, still not saying a word.

In no time Maine and Eric unwantingly rush to Arieus's aide.

Tuesday

Eric and Maine slowly walk down the chilling basement. This time they are around the corner from Arieus's cell, there is a tad bit more space but the conditions remain still the same.

"You see that game last night? I told you my Cowboys wont nothing to fuck with," says Maine excitedly as he follows behind Eric.

"Naw," Eric mumbles.

"That shit was live. Prescott took them boys for a ride, 5 touchdowns, Zero interceptions. And you know my boy Touchdown Dez did his thing. Boy that shit was crazy. I swear it's a Holliday every time we beat them weak ass Deadskins."

"Yeah," Eric mumbles once more.

"Man what they fuck that bitch do now? Yall was just good the yesterday."

"Nigga who ever said she did something," says Eric before stopping in his tracks, grabbing Maine by the arm as the two men stare face to face. "And foreal bro I'm not in the mood for you to be disrespecting my girl. I thought I told your ass bout that shit,"

"Maaaan. Shut that soft ass shit up. Damn. You been good. What the fuck she do now? Matter of a fact. I don't even care. I washed my hands with your ass," says Maine before removing Eric's hand and making his way back down the hallway, now leading the way.

"What? Nigga, aint nobody ask you to care," spits Eric as he too continues to walk.

"Man you better lower your fucking tone," says Maine, turning around as he spoke.

"Nigga. Who is you? I don't gotta lower shit. You got me fucked up."

"Naw nigga you got me fucked up."

"Fuck you."

"Nigga Fuck you."

"You a bitch."

"Nigga you a bitch."

"Show me I'm a bitch," says Maine, turning around, chest poked, fist clinched as he and Eric stand chest to chest before Eric's anger gets the best of him and he decides to shove Maine. Unable to hold back Maine quickly tosses Eric against the wall, where he immediately falls to the floor. Dropping along with him Maine slams his open hand onto Eric's neck, furiously choking life from him. "Listen here nigga. I don't know what the fuck happened to you last night. But I'm tired of this shit. Nigga this the shit females do. Any problem you got at home, leave that shit the fuck at home. I hate to do this but I'm sick of that shit," says Maine, sternly before a tear falls from Eric's face. "Nigga hell you crying for?" he asks before releasing him, backing away as Eric continues to sit on the ground. "I know I aint that strong."

"Man Bro. It's Shwanda," Eric whines, wiping away his tear. "You know I do everything for her. Every decision I make I think

17

about how it would effect her. My nigga how many times I had to tell you she got fired from another job?" he asks looking up to Maine.

"Plenty."

"Yeah nigga. And even when she knows I worked a double I still gotta come home and cook and clean," says Eric before standing to his feet. "Nigga I never get massages, compliments, nothing. Man to tell the truth she only gives me pussy when she gets horny. She just does what the fuck she wants and I let her," Eric complains as he straightens himself up as he and Maine both began to walk.

"So why you with her?" Maine asks.

"Man I don't know. I guess I love her too much. Man I never met anybody who makes me feel like she does. I can't even explain it dog. It's crazy. I love her more than I love myself," says Eric before dropping his head.

"Bro. Come on dog. How does that sound?"

"I know man. But it's the truth."

"Bro just look at yourself. Look how she's got you acting."

"Who you telling. But that's not even what's got me fucked up this morning. You know my Mom birthday was yesterday."

"Yeah, you told me."

"Mind you, I've been telling Shwanda about this for weeks. It was really important to my Mom that everybody came to her crib for a little diner. Not to mention my Moms always been there for her and looking out."

"Ok.Ok," says Maine as they keep on stepping.

18

"So how about its time to go, I'm getting dressed and shit and I look to the living room couch and this bitch chillin in her underwear talking bout she not feeling too good. So like a dumbass I run to the store and get orange juice and medicine. Come back, give it to her and leave. Man I come home after my Moms diner around 11, get in the crib and this bitch getting ready to hit the club."

"Oh hell naw," Maine exclaimed. "I know you snapped."

"Damn right! I went the fuck off. Got so mad I punched a damn whole in the wall and everything. But you think that helped?"

"Hell naw," answers Maine.

"You know it didn't. She still went out and she aint pull back up till I was leaving for work. I aint get a wink of fucking sleep. Texting her dumbass all night. Dog, I hate my life," he said as they approached a metal door that reads 'Boiler Room'.

Maine whips out his set of keys. "Well bro you already know what my advice is," he says as he opens the door.

Wasting no time, Pete yells. "Yall niggas got me in this lil ass room burning up for beating a damn child murders ass. Yall aint shit." Looking inside the room, there's nothing but a mat on the floor along with a cup that appears to have been urinated in. "I gotta shit like a motherfucker. I should sue the fuck outta yall niggas," says Pete as he throws his hands in front of him to be cuffed.

"Dog you act like you weren't fighting," Eric replies as he slams the cuff onto Pete's wrists. "In the predicament you're in we could have easily ruined everything you got going on. But we didn't," says Eric.

19

"And hold on, first of all, like we've been telling you "We" aint have you nowhere. Nigga all we do is take yall where yall need to be and make sure yall in order. Don't blame us for shit," says Maine as the three walk back down the hallway.

"Second of all. How you gon call somebody a murderer. If my memory serves me right. You're appealing a murder and countless other crimes as we speak," follows Eric.

"What? Nigga I aint Murder shit," Pete says looking over to Eric. "Man I thought you was cool. You be acting like a straight bitch sometimes," says Pete aggressively.

"You know I can get your ass sent back to the boiler room," follows Eric.

"Man what the fuck kind of bitch ass shit you on? Nigga I'm a young black man just like you," Pete says before looking over to Maine. "Ay Man whatsup with your homeboy?"

"Man you know how he is."

"Women problems again?" Asks Pete.

Maine bursts out laughing. "Yo. You been down in the basement by yourself for a month and you already know about his problems. That's a damn shame," he says as he looks over to Eric in disappointment.

"Nigga who don't know. I heard Shwanda be dogging your ass out," says Pete as Maine continues to laugh, causing Eric to snap, charging Pete, before Maine quickly holds him back.

"Chill bro. Chill," states Maine.

"Man fuck this nigga. I aint tryna here this shit from a worthless piece of shit like you, nigga you aint never gonna see the light of day."

"Man fuck you," screams Pete as he steps to Eric's face.

"Naw fuck you."

"Yo yall niggas chill," says Maine as he separates the two. "Come on," he says motioning for them to proceed walking. They walk but not before one last stare down.

"Why am I even wasting my time with you? I'm sure you'll be back to getting fucked soon enough from them inmates in the Penitentiary. Think you're going home? Motherfucker you aint going nowhere. See, I might be having women problems but at least I actually get to go home and see mine," says Eric as Pete walks in front, never looking back. "How's it feel to know you'll never get a piece of pussy again in your life, bitch. Yeah, someone's probably at your baby mama's crib dogging that sweet pussy out right now as we speak."

Continuing to walk Pete takes a deep breath before speaking. "See my brother, I been away for almost three years," he says, still staring straight ahead. "In the beginning I probably would've spit in your face for saying some shit like that to me. But I'm at peace with my situation. I don't care what you say, I'm getting out of here. Simple as that. God got me."

"Yeah that's what they all say. Just try to worry bout your own situation and don't worry about mine."

"Man how do you deal with this soft ass nigga all day?" asks Pete, looking back to Maine, who walks a few steps behind him.

Maine shakes his head. "It's hard."

"If I aint know no better I'd think he's the one in the slammer. Always mad at the world and shit," replies Pete as they turn a familiar corner where their space is once again limited. "Yo where the fuck all taking me?" asks Pete as a drop of water splashes onto his head from above. "My old cell?"

"Yep," replies Eric.

"Yall got that motherfucking bitch ass Police nigga outta there yet?" he asks, looking back as neither Eric nor Maine say a word. "Oh hell naw," Pete blurts as they approach the cell, where Arieus is laying face up, on the top bunk staring at the ceiling. "Why the fuck y'all still got him in here? Is yall crazy or something?"

"What I tell you about that 'yall' shit," Maine interrupts. "I aint got nothing to do with where they put you. Just following orders," he says as he whips out his set of keys.

"Fuck! They always tryna keep me in a position to get in trouble. I'm just tryna do my time and work on my appeal and get the fuck home."

"Then do that," says Maine.

"Nigga you ever been caged up with a person you hate for 23 hours a day? Huh?" Pete asks, switching his attention back and forward between Eric and Maine as both correctional officer stand unfazed?

22

"Yeah I aint think so," says Pete as he stares into the cell, chest inflating in and out.

"Well they got us on post watching y'all all day. So if you need us we'll be down the hall," says Maine, opening the cell once again.

"Fuck y'all." says Pete as he steps in. "This some bullshit," he follows before sliding his hands through the chuck hold, where Maine releases him from the cuffs as Eric stands behind smiling. "Fuck you," Pete says directed to Eric before turning, removing his jail issued orange jumpsuit, exposing his white tee shirt and matching white boxer shorts before flopping down onto his bunk. "Yall just want me to catch another murder," Pete screams as Maine and Eric walk away.

"Yo you better not do that pissing shit again. I swear, if I smell even the slightest bit of piss I'll be forced to beat your motherfucking ass. Don't look at me. Don't even breathe my way," Pete yells looking up to the top bunk as if he could see through it.

Still Arieus doesn't speak.

"Yeah you don't got to say shit. And you better not try nothing funny while I'm asleep. I been doing this jail since I was 14. I can sleep with one eye open. So don't even try that revenge shit."

Arieus still remains silent.

Pete hops up. "Aye nigga. Yo, I aint gon take no more of your disrespect. Aint no nigga just gonna ignore me. You only pulling that shit cause you know I can't do nothing bout it," Pete says emotionally pointing his finger towards Arieus as spit particles fly out of his mouth.

"I fucking hate you," Pete yells as Arieus looks over nonchalantly, still not an ounce of fear visible. "Nigga didn't I say don't look at me. Fuck you," says Pete as he flops back onto his bed. "I don't give a fuck if you talk or not. I hate your bitch ass anyway. I can't believe they got me in here, no T.V. no radio. With a fucking cold blooded murderer. Yo how the fuck you kill a 16 year old? What the fuck was going on in your brain? How do you even sleep? Like, you gotta be a bitch ass nigga. What you was scared of a little kid or something? You know your bitch ass supposed to be doing time just like any other murderer. But because you a damn Police officer they want to give you a break. You know you did that shit on purpose. I hate you," Pete yells. "You know you going to hell right? Hope the devil stick his damn thorns up your ass," Pete rants before closing his eyes, once again tossing and turning until he finally falls asleep.

About 4 hours later he's awoken.

"Ay nigga get up," bolts Maine from outside the cell, awakening both Pete and Arieus.

24

"You know you aint going nowhere," Eric says to Arieus. "You know we don't need you. We talking to the angry nigga," he says looking down at Arieus.

"Fuck you," says Pete as he stretches his arms. "Hell y'all need me for?"

"They say your lawyers here to talk to you," replies Maine.

"Bet. Damn right," says Pete as he hops out of bed.

"Don't get too excited it's just a 5 minute meeting." Follows Eric.

"Yall niggas aint never been on lock down before. I'm about to cherish the hell outta these 5 minutes," he says as he slips into his jumper and shoes before walking over to the gate, sliding his hands through the chuck hold to be cuffed.

After cuffing him, Maine opens the gate before shutting it as Pete steps out into the cramped hallway.

"Yo you good now? You look a little better than earlier," Pete asks Eric as he exits the cell and leads the way down the hallway.

"Nigga I'm always good," Eric replies.

"You better tell that lie to someone who doesn't know you," says Pete.

"Motherfucker fuck you. You don't know me. But if y'all nosey mo'fuckers really would like to know. Yeah I'm good. I'm real good," he says as a huge smile takes over his face.

"He went home at lunch, they must've fucked," says Maine to Pete.

"Fucked," exclaims Eric berfore bursting into laughter. "Nigga we don't fuck. That's childish. We make love. Real love. Our shit Deep. After we were finished we just laid there staring in each others eyes before I got back dressed for work," says Eric, reminiscing. "I aint even have time for a shower. Here smell my finger. I know you aint smell nothing like this in a while," he says as he steps up, thrusting his finger into Pete's face.

"Move nigga," screams Pete.

"Hold on, first of all let me ask you this. Did she use a butt plug or something cause you sounding fruity as a bitch," asks Maine.

"Fuck you," replies Eric.

"And second, what could she possible complain to you about. Yo ass don't do shit but kiss her ass and take care of her."

"Naw man. I do things she doesn't like. She says I complain a lot and it makes her feel like a bad girlfriend."

"Nigga she is a bad girlfriend," Maine exclaims. "You got all the reasons in the world to complain, shit, you probably aint doing enough complaining if you ask me."

Pete and Maine both laugh as Maine presses the up button for the elevator. The door instantly opens.

"Hell you laughing bout. You always got some type of input but I bet all your girls was whores," Eric says, directing his anger to Pete as they step inside the elevator.

"Boy you must don't know who the fuck I am. Don't get me wrong I done ran through plenty whores in my day. But I can honestly say my main girl most definitely wasn't a hoe. Sharee's the furthest thing from it actually," says Pete as Maine presses '3'.

"Nigga that's what they all say. I'll bet my last dollar since you got locked up she done joined the BDC," says Eric.

"BIG DICK CLUB," Eric and Maine both say in unison.

"Ay I'm sure she did," Pete responds, shrugging his shoulders. "I can't be mad at her. I been gone for a minute. I was sentenced to 181 years. I could care less about that. What I do care about is the fact that she's on her way to graduating college. My son has everything he wants. She puts money on my books. Visits me so my son can see me and most importantly she answers that motherfucking phone. So for the "Big Dick Club" in my eyes maybe she deserves it." He winks his eyes at the C.O.'s who are left speechless as the elevator door opens.

"Ay what did you say her name was again," asks Maine, jokingly.

"Fuck you," replies Pete.

"I'm just saying. Just in case you don't get out your situation she might need a nigga like me. And I damn sure need a girl like her," Maine states as they step out of the elevator.

"Sorry bro but you a little too ugly for her taste," fires back Pete as the three men switch over to serious mode. No longer are they alone. This floor is completely different. Fellow C.O's and other shackled inmates walk amongth them causing the mood to stiffen as they make their way down the somber hallway.

It doesn't take long at all to reach the room in which Pete's lawyer awaits him. Opening the door for Pete, Maine uncuff's him as he whispers one last thing before Pete walks in. "And about that little comment about me being ugly. I don't know if you've heard, I know you've been locked up for a while. But sorry my nigga. Ugly is the new cute," he says as Pete walks in.

"Yeah right," Pete whispers before redirecting his attention to his White middle aged lawyer, Steven Simmons. His black and white hair is slicked back as he sits draped in a tailored three piece suit. His legs are crossed and his foot can't seem to stop swinging from left to right as his index finger rapidly beats the table. He struggles to crack a smile as Pete addresses him, "How you doing Mr. Simmons?"

28

"What's up Pete? How's everything?" asks Mr. Simmons.

"Everything's alright. Whatsup. I know it's gotta be something big for you to Show up today. Let me know something. Good news or bad?" asks Pete eagerly before taking a seat across from Steven. "Whatsup. I'm grown. Whatsup?" Pete asks after Mr. Simmons throws his head into his hands, covering his face.

"Sho's dead," whispers Mr. Simmons.

"What? Huh? How? I thought he was in witness protection," Pete, disappointingly screams.

"Yeah supposedly he got out and went back to his old ways. Only this time he wasn't King Sho the O.G. anymore. He was Albert Thomas and no one respects Albert Thomas. So, I guess one thing led to another and the gangsters in the little small town he was living in, killed him," says, Mr. Simmons, looking away as he speaks.

"Killed him? What the fuck," Pete asks, throwing his head back in disbelief. "So what does that mean for my case? How am I gonna prove that he's the one who killed Officer McNair and that he was the leader of the Warriors if he's dead? You think we got a chance?" Pete asks, hopefully.

"We can try."

"We can try? Fuck," he shouts. "Just last week you was saying you had scooped up enough witnesses and dirt on Sho to turn this whole case around and get me and my nigga Trell out. Whatsup?"

"Yeah. I still do. I just don't know how well the Appeal will go without him. I'm just trying to be honest with you Pete."

"Honest? Nigga I'm the one being honest. It's not like I'm making shit up. Everything I tell your ass is true," Pete says before taking a deep breath. "Look man, you told me I was about to be a free man or at least get out in a few years. You damn near guaranteed me. I got 178 years left bro. You gotta find me a way outta here. You just got too," said Pete, slamming his hand to the table."

"I'm gonna try my hardest."

"Try! Try! Nigga my life on the line. My fucking life," Pete yells as he punches his right hand into his left palm. "Aint no try. Matter of a fact. Fuck it. I'ma find a way myself," says Pete as he stands to his feet, storming over to the door before banging his fists onto it. "C.O.," he yells before looking back hatefully at the lawyer. "C.O.!"

Eric and Maine arrive quickly before cuffing Pete once again and quietly escorting him back down to his basement home.

"Bad news?" Eric asks as they enter the elevator.

Pete doesn't speak back.

"Man leave that nigga alone. You worrisome as hell," Maine replies, shaking his head at Eric.

"Leave him alone? He didn't just leave me alone. Fuck that," Eric barks back.

"Come on man. Give the guy a break. You don't know what just happened in that room. Don't be like that," says Maine as the elevator door re opens.

"What? Yall was just calling me soft for loving my girl," replies Eric as the three step out of the elevator, making their way back to Pete's cell. "But this nigga aint soft because he's mad about a situation he put himself in."

"Chill bro," says Maine.

"Man fuck that, I'ma speak my mind just like he was a few minutes ago. Ima keep it real. Niggas wanna be gangsters. Niggas wanna be thugs. Robbing and stealing, selling drugs. But then wanna be sorry when shit hits the fan. I don't mean any harm but I don't feel sorry for none of you motherfuckers."

Heated sweat oozes down Pete's stress riddled face as he leads the pack down the hallway.

"Man you don't even know if the nigga even did whatever he's in here for," say Maine.

"It don't matter. I do know that I believe in God and Karma. So even if his ass aint do it. He did something in life to deserve this. God don't make mistakes. Simple as that. He deserves this."

In a flash Pete turns around, colliding his head forcefully against Eric's.

Surprised, Eric falls to the ground but not before dragging Pete along with him. Still, enraged, Pete sinks his teeth into the side of Eric's arm like a starving piranha as Eric screams in torturous pain.

To the rescue, Maine frantically breaks up the fight, pulling Pete from on top of Eric, mistakenly allowing Eric to land a sucker punch to the side of Pete's face. "Bitch ass nigga," Pete screams as he attempts to break free of Maine's grip tight grasp.

"Yall calm down," shouts Maine as he continues to drag Pete away.

"Oh yeah. You wanna play like that. I got something for you bitch," says Eric as his shaking hands reach to his side for his walky talky before realizing during the scuffle it had slid down the hall. Wasting no time he stands to his feet, darting over to retrieve it.

"Bro no," screams Maine as Eric races to the opposite end from where he and Pete stood.

"Naw fuck it," blurts Pete as blood trickles from his mouth. "Call back up. Send me to the Hole, to the boiler room. I don't give a fuck bout shit. I'm bouta give them a reason to really give me life," Pete blurts still trying to break from Maine's grasp.

"You damn right I'ma send your lil bitch ass to the Hole," Eric says, finally grabbing the walky talky.

32

"Naw bro don't do it. You say you believe in God. Forgive him man. Put yourself in his shoes," says Maine as he continues holding Pete back.

"His shoes? I would never be in his shoes. I wake up at the crack of dawn every day to come here. I deliver Pizza's on the weekend. You think I wouldn't love to live the glamourous life? Being a drug dealer. Huh? I'm pretty sure his young ass made more a day than I made in a month. But you want me to feel sorry for him and kiss his ass. No. Fuck no," blurts Eric, using his hands as he talks. "Like I said, you do the crime you do the time."

"Fuck," Pete screams, finally breaking away from Maine's Grasp, falling to his knees. "Fuck. Fuck everything. Kill me nigga. Kill me. What I gotta do to make you kill me," he screams louder.

Maine and Eric, look down at Pete, both staring silently.

"I don't give a fuck bout shit. I aint got shit and I'm never gonna have shit. I'm fucking stuck in this bitch forever. This aint fucking living," he continues screaming before yelling even louder than before. "Kill me. Kill me," he shouts.

"Calm down bro," says Maine.

"Calm down? Calm down?" Pete repeats, never looking back to Maine. "Nigga I been in this shit since I was 18. My life is fucked up, every night for the past couple year I been hearing niggas sharpening knifes, screams from niggas getting raped." Pete says as he tilts his head to the ceiling. "Not to mention I was locked up for some shit I aint do for 3 years before that. You think I deserve that?" he asks looking over to Eric. "Huh motherfucker? You telling me I fucking deserve that?"

Eric looks away, seeming unsure of what to say.

"Maybe I do," says Pete, dropping his head. "Shit, I don't know. But all my life all I've seen is Pain. And to tell the truth. I don't know what it is but that whole God thing is becoming one big ass joke to me. Life don't love nobody, especially me. Got my son and my girl out there all by themselves. Got me all by myself. What the fuck kind of God would do that? If you ask me I'm starting to feel like it aint one," cries Pete, still looking down at the damp floor.

Eric and Maine look over to one another.

"Kill me. Kill me," Pete screams once again.

"Chill bro. Chill, just try to chill out," responds Maine.

"Yeah man. My bad. I was just in my feelings cause you were clowning me earlier," Eric says looking down to Pete, who's head is still lowered. "I'm sorry man. I definitely took it too far."

Suddenly Pete's body drops to the ground flat, arms cuffed in front of him as he lays sobbing while Maine and Eric remained still, watching. After about a minute, Pete slowly stands to his feet, wiping away his tears with his shoulder. "Man if you aint gon kill me just take me to my cell," he says softly, head to the sky.

Without saying a word the three men walk slowly back to the cell, Eric in front.

Upon their arrival Pete enters the cell still never making eye contact.

As Maine and Eric depart after uncuffing him, he removes his jumper and lays across his rack as Arieus stares up at the ceiling. Once again tears flow down Pete's cheek as sadness takes control of his face. In no time the pain grows unbearable and Pete drifts off to sleep.

Wednesday

"Chow," screams Maine awakening Pete and Arieus. Without so much as a word Pete stands up to retrieve his tray of grits, sausage, folded egg and a small cup of sweet tea, while Arieus lays still.

Maine and Eric don't say a word. They calmly walk away as Pete sits back on his bed, eating his food slowly, seemingly forcing himself.

After finishing he stands to his feet, tossing his tray between the chuck hold onto the outside hallway.

As Arieus lays face up staring blankly at the ceiling, Pete looks over to him.

"Man," says Pete as a chip from the cracked ceiling falls onto Arieus's face. "My bad bout beating your ass. I just felt like I had to do it," Pete says looking over to Arieus. "I mean, you did kill a black kid and I truly can't understand for the life of me why you would do some stupid shit like that. But I was laying here thinking a lot last night and at the end of the day, I'm not God. I can't judge you. Shit, I been getting judged since I was 14 years old. And for some shit I aint even do. And you know the crazy thing. Maybe that was just a test. I know I'm talking your head off," Pete says before laying back down on his bunk in the same position Arieus laid in. "Shit you probably aint even listening, but fuck it, this the closest thing I've ever had to

36

counseling in a long time. I damn sure need it," says Pete as she shakes his head. "When I was 14 I saw my favorite person in the world kill a man right in front of my eyes. And what's so crazy is, I'm the one who went to jail for it. 14 years old dog. But I did exactly what I was taught. I didn't say shit. Yeah, I eventually beat the charge. I used to always justify it by saying that if I had snitched it wouldn't benefit anyone. But I've been thinking. Maybe I should've said something. Maybe the Karma from what I witnessed is what has me in the situation I'm in now. Or maybe it's the fact that I helped ruin all them other young niggas life by influencing them to be in a gang. But yo, I swear I aint know shit was gon turn out the way it did. But damn. Do I really deserve all this? I really didn't fully understand what I was doing. Shit. I was teenager. I guess I knew it wasn't right but Sho was like my Dad. I would've never betrayed him. But boy did he betray me. I guess he finally got what he deserved but look where it leaves me," Pete says before taking a breath. "That shit taught me so much and my dumbass still confused. It's like so many thoughts that run through my head a day. I can hardly focus on anything. I got a fucking son out there man. And my dumbass wait 3 years before I even agree to snitch on Sho about the murder and everything else he's done. My loyalty just wouldn't allow me to do it. After all this time this nigga still had mind control over me. Now look at me, it's possible that I can tell the truth and still get the time. I know these judges really don't give a damn who really did all that shit. In their eyes we're all the same," Pete says before pausing. "Shit really getting to me man. I'd hate to tell the truth for nothing and go back to the Feds being known as Pete the Snitch. The only reason I even been surviving in Prison is because everybody respect me as some so called real nigga. Shit would be cool if I was free but being labeled a snitch in there could get me killed in that bitch. Shits crazy, I'm lost, I aint gonna kill myself but I swear I wouldn't mind if someone killed me," Pete says before pausing again appearing to be fighting back more tears.

"I know the feeling," says Arieus, in a low deep tone.

"What? You talking?" Pete asks, confused.

"Yeah. You may not believe me. But the way you're feeling right now. The feeling of being trapped with no control over your life is a feeling that I'm all too familiar with. It's probably the feeling that I know more than anything else," says Arieus, still staring at the ceiling.

"What you mean?"

"See, the world doesn't know me. Doesn't know anything about me. Yeah you guys might think you do, but I swear you have no fucking clue."

"Well then nigga fill me in. We aint got shit but time."

Arieus sits silent for about a minute before speaking. "I'm going to let you know right now, when I'm done. You won't look at me the same. Either you'll hate me more or you'll understand me. Either way I don't care to be honest. I don't know why, but for the first time I'm ready to talk. I just gotta let some shit off. I've been holding shit in for far too long. Its time."

"Well what the hell you waiting for?" asks Pete.

_1985_

Norfolk, Va. 1985. The Lakers were world champions, Ronald Reagan was President of the United States but more importantly to this story, Arieus Hatch was born. Some people make ill decisions that cause their life's journey to become tragic. But for Arieus, an existence filled with far more negatives than positives was pretty much destined. Ever since the moment his Mom, Jalisa laid on the couch clutching her stomach in pain, dude's life was nothing short of a roller coaster. Actually comparing his life to a roller coaster may be a tad misinforming. Roller Coasters tend to have twist and turns, occasionally springing up. This was far different than Arieus's life, maybe the best comparison to his upbringing may be a water slide, or better yet a Bunje jump, minus the bunje.

"**AAAAHH**," screamed Jalisa, as she curled up into a ball on the couch of her living room.

Tim, her young stereotypical trailer park trash baby's daddy flies in the room, clutching a beer can stumbling over dirty clothes, magazines and oversized roaches. "Oh shit. Is it time?" he blurts as Jalisa uncomfortably nods in pain. "Oh Shit," Tim repeats as he runs back into the bedroom while Jalisa continues moaning. "AHH fuck." He screams.

"What's wrong baby?" Jalisa struggles to ask.

"I dropped my fucking beer. That was my last God Damn one. Fuck," he screams. "I'm pissed the fuck off. It was damn near full," he whines. "Shit."

"It's ok baby. We can pick up one on the way to the hospital," she says as if she was using everything she had inside to release her words.

"It's ok. I'll drop you off first," he says as he returns with a baby bag thrown across his shoulder. "Come on baby," he urges as he assists Jalisa from the couch. "I'm about to have a son," he shouts as they rush out of the house.

Once outside their quickly greeted by dozens of their fellow Trailer Park Neighbors, who are all sitting outside in beach chairs enjoying the July weather, gossiping about everything from Elvis to who the Top Racer of the time was. During this year it was a tossup between Dale Earnhardt and Darrell Waltrip.

After exchanging hello's and assuring a couple drunk friends that Tim was indeed sober enough to make it to the hospital, the young couple headed out in Tim's most prized possession, his 1978 Ford F150.

"I love you," says Tim as they dangerously back out of their dirt driveway.

"I love you more baby," she follows back as Tim leans over for a passionate kiss.

As they speed down the road, Tim discovers a surprise on the driver's side floor. An old beer he'd forgotten to drink earlier. His night couldn't get any better. He cracks open his beverage, cranks up 'Lynyrd Skynyrd's Sweet Home Alabama', and joyfully sings to the top of his lungs before looking over to Jalisa once again. "Baby I can't believe I'm about to have a baby boy. He's gonna play football. I'm gonna teach him about girls. How to swim, fish, camp. Ah man," he says before pausing and looking dead into Jalisa's eyes. "And you know we're getting married right."

"Really baby?" says Jalisa excitedly as her eyes sparkle with delight.

"Ya damn skippy we are. Shits about to change around here. I know I been in and out of the joint since we met but I'm done with that shit. I swear I'm done. Its time I grew up. I know I said that when we had Amanda but I'm serious now. I gotta show my son what a real man is. Ya know. You're about to meet a brand new Tim," he states never taking his eyes away from Jalisa.

"That's great baby," follows Jalisa, breathing heavily. "But I think we forgot something," she says to Tim as he finally puts his eyes back on the road.

"What baby?" he asks looking over once again.

"Amanda," shouts Jalisa.

"Oh shit," Tim yells as he quickly makes a screeching U-turn in the middle of the street, not wasting a second.

Racing home, he arrives in no time, hops out, car still running, rushing in to retrieve his forgotten two year old daughter. With all the excitement she'd somehow slipped both parents mind.

"How'd your Mom forget you?" asked Tim to Amanda as he picks her up. "I'm drunk, at least I got an excuse, what's hers?"

At only two, of course Amanda had no reply, so instead, her bright hazel eyes simply stared at Tim, smiling showing the new teeth she'd acquired before letting him know exactly how she felt, throwing up all over his white tank top. Now any other day Tim would be mad. But not that day. No sir, it was too good of a day. His baby boy was arriving. Nothing could knock him off of his high horse. Or so he thought.

Darting back out of the house Tim tosses Amanda into the arms of 'Michelle', the neighborhood designated babysitter. She wasn't really fit for the position considering her love for alcohol and prescription drugs but she was unemployed and never left the house, not to mention, free. Choosing her to watch the kids was a sort of no brainer for most.

Arriving in record time, the couple burst through the hospital doors, where Tim makes sure everyone around knew that his son was set to make his first appearance, ignorantly shouting, "Hey

Motherfuckers my sons about to be born. Somebody get my ol lady to a room right fucking now and I mean it."

Somehow his obnoxious attitude got the job done and he and his future wife were signed in and ready for delivery. After hours of impatiently waiting, it seemed as if the moment they'd dreamed of was seconds away from coming into fruition.

While the head Dr. Leon Robinson and his crew coached Jalisa along, Tim on the other hand was unable to join in on the moment. Instead he chose a much further position in the corner of the small room. Draped in hospital gear he stood nervously biting his finger nails through his latex gloves thinking of how this day had finally come.

Growing up he had never thought of having a black son. Actually he would have probably shot himself had he known he'd ever do something so foolish. But after being cheated on by white trash after white trash he had slowly lost faith in his female race.

Not too long after, there walks Jalisa into his life. Like Tim, she would have never thought of dating a white man either, but she kind of had the same story as Tim. After a life fit for a Tyler Perry Film she too gave up on her race in matters of relationships. She needed something different, something fresh. So when she spotted Tim stroll into 'Cheetah's Gentleman Club', tall, blonde, good looking and not to mention a smile that could woo any woman of any ethnic descent, she made it her duty to give him the greatest lap dance, her young 18 years old self could give.

After grinding for free for damn near an hour, Tim finally popped the question. "What are you doing when you get out of here?" he asked as he gently caressed her vagina.

"You. If I'm lucky," she replied.

In the beginning, the two both had second thoughts about their newly found romance. Being stared at and judged wherever you go can have a profound effect on a couple. Soon they were both looking for a way out of love. Only there was no escape, in no time something as simple as the presence of one another had become an addiction far too powerful to fight.

In Tim, Jalisa saw a strong man, and not just any strong man. A white strong man. All of her life it had seemed as though white men had control over the earth. So with Tim she figured, the closer she stood by him the more control she would have over her own life and just maybe things would finally go her way.

While Tim on the other hand had quickly understood the phrase once you go black you don't go back. The sex was amazing. By far the best his little white penis had ever had. But that wasn't even the kicker. Wanting desperately to be accepted into Tim's white world Jalisa did any and everything he asked. The word 'No' was nonexistent in reguards to him. In her eyes he was God, which was just how Tim always wanted to be acknowledged.

45

Growing up he'd always been looked upon by his white counterparts as less than. In his head he always felt like he wasn't a 'Real White Man'. He didn't speak well, never did well in school, and worse of all, he was poor. Jalisa changed all of that. Worshiping the ground he walked on, his sense of self-worth skyrocketed through the roof. With each day, soon it wasn't Jalisa who he was addicted to anymore. It was the feeling of importance. There was no way in hell he was letting her out of his site.

After months of creeping around it was finally time to come clean and break the news to his friends and family in the Trailer Park. He no longer gave a rat's ass on how they felt about him dating a Nigger.

It took a while but with time Jalisa had quit her job as a dancer and was dwelling in the 'Lake Shaw Park Trailer Homes' with her man. Besides a few initial stares and cold shoulders she soon fit in perfectly. Or as perfect as she could.

Jalisa had a special quality in her, despite the hardships life had dealt her, she still held on to a certain sweetness that couldn't be denied by the most brutal of Klan members. Her wide smile and bright eyes sometimes hypnotized the whites into thinking she was one of the good ones.

Soon Amanda was born and they moved from Tim's family Trailer, to their own spot a few feet up the lot. Besides the dysfunction of living in a low income trailer, life seemed to be going great. Notice the word 'Seemed'.

"Push," Dr. Leon bolts as Jalisa screams in obvious pain. "We're almost there. Keep going," He urges as Jalisa's screams grow louder. "I think we got him. Keep Pushing. Keep Pushing."

Then it happened, Arieus's, bald baby's head pops out screaming at the site of the world that would torture him for years to come.

"We got him," says The Dr. as he removes Arieus's entire body from his former residence.

The smile on Tim is Priceless as he ventures away from his corner to take a closer peek at his long awaited baby boy. His bliss wouldn't last long. In the blink of an eye his face turned upside down and a Devilish glare replaced his once pleasant expression. "That aint my damn baby," he shouted.

Uh oh. Just when Tim thought Jalisa was different. Just when he thought things in life were looking up and he'd finally had everything he'd dreamed upon for so long, a piercing dagger was struck through his heart.

His boy who he'd raise with that lucky black blood floating through his veins, his boy who he hoped would be able to think like the white man but ball like the black boys. His boy he was going to take fishing, teach about the birds and the bee's, how to change oil and just do everything his alcoholic father never did with him. His boy, may have turned out to not be his boy.

Ok, Jalisa was a brown skinned black woman and of course Tim was white. Arieus on the other hand came out probably as dark as any baby could be. Looking at him, it was clear as day that the type of complexion he was born with was the result of two black people coming together. No doubt.

As Tim visibly grew enraged, all eyes focused on him as the mood suddenly became dark as horns seemed to sprout from his scalp and pencil sized veins appeared throughout his face and neck.

Before he could be restrained Tim forced his way past the nurses and Dr.'s in route to choke the life from Jalisa, as the room went into a frenzy. Together, everyone desperately attempted to remove Tim's hulk like hands from Jalisa's throat, only nothing seemed to work.

"Security," they all scream as Tim's 'Anger' meter rose.

After what seemed like forever two large security guards rushed into the room grabbing Tim, still unable to pull him off. He yelled, "I'ma Kill you bitch. Whore. You bitch. I'ma kill you," before finally being tazered to the ground.

Baby Arieus screams, still attached to the umbilical cord as Jalisa regains her breath to plead with her seemingly insane boyfriend. "Baby I'm sorry. Baby I'm sorry," she cries, gasping for air.

48

As he's dragged out of the room, shaking and trembling Tim still manages to slip out the words, "Fuck you. I'ma kill you Bitch."

Unable to think straight Jalisa somehow musters up enough strength to hop out of bed, chasing after her man, only to plummet to the floor as Baby Arieus, falls hard along with her.

"Damn my nigga. That's crazy as hell. That shit really happened?" asks Pete hopping up from his rack to look Arieus face to face.

"Of course," says Arieus still staring at the ceiling. "Of course I don't actually remember but from the stories I've always heard. Yeah, that's exactly how it went down."

"Damn so that nigga Tim really wont your Pops?" asks Pete.

"Let me ask you this. Do I look like I have a white Dad?"

"Damn. You're right. That's crazy," says Pete, shaking his head in disbelief. "So hold on. Did you ever find out who your real Pops was?"

"Nope. I guess his last name was Hatch. I don't know. All I know is that's my last name and it wasn't my Mom's or Tim's."

"You meant to tell me you aint never ask?"

"Nope. I never really asked too many questions growing up. From what I discovered during the countless arguments around the house was basically, Tim was back and forth to jail a lot and during one of those times my Mom fucked around with some black guy and voila, here I am."

"Hold on. What the fuck you mean arguments? So you telling me that they stayed together after that crazy ass shit?"

"Yep"

"Why? What the fuck. That nigga Tim was trippin. If my girl ever did some shit like that I would've been gone forever. Fuck her, fuck you, shit, fuck my daughter too. I woulda had to move to a whole other country or something. No offence bro but that shit is foul. Not to mention embarrassing as hell."

"Yeah I suppose it is. But I kind of have an inkling as to why he decided to stay."

"Why?" asked Pete, curiously.

"Simple. My Mom was a dumb bitch."

"Damn bro that's a little harsh aint it. I mean I know what she did was wrong but damn, she's still your Mama," says Pete still standing to his feet.

"Like I said. My Mom was a dumb bitch and he knew he would be able to walk all over her for life. Why would he leave something like that? He was a dumb man. But he apparently wasn't that dumb."

1993

Bright and sunny day, birds are chirping, leaves are swinging from the trees. You couldn't ask for a better backdrop for Tim and Jalisa's backyard wedding. All of the kids are in attendance. A lot has changed though. It's not just Amanda and Arieus anymore, Faith and Grace have now been added to the equation.

They're Tim and Jalisa's 3 year old twins. After the whole baby being born black fiasco, Tim was determined to have a boy. Therefore he relentlessly tried over and over, year after year, still, each time it was the same results, another girl.

Feeling no emotional connection, Tim demanded each bundle of so called joy be shipped off to the nearest adoption agency. Of course Jalisa wasn't too fond of his brash decisions but as always, she had no say so.

Over the years Tim had become worse than ever. Can't say if it was the drinking that was causing his extreme heartlessness but whatever it was had completely taken over. If it weren't for the fact that Tim had always held a weird fascination with twins, Faith and Grace too would have been thrown by the waste side.

But back to the story at hand. The wedding's small, non-traditional to say the least. Not a single man in dress shoes, nope, not a loafer in site. Honestly it kind of appeared as if all of the men had slipped on the shoes they'd cut the grass or had taken out the trash in the day before. You have to give them some credit though, at least they decided to throw on their Sunday's best. Yeah, they might have forgotten to iron them, and they could have stood to at least try to match, but hey, at least they tried.

As far as the opposite sex was concerned, the women did all manage to iron their noticeably thrifty dresses and pant suits. Now when it comes to their heels, let's just say they weren't as new as one might hope. Most appeared to have been passed down from generation to generation. Throughout the event it wasn't anything to see a woman struggling to keep her balance due to the fact that one heel seemed to be a little taller than the other. Still, they never seemed to be bothered. They carried themselves with as much class and dignity as they possessed.

A poor sense of style wasn't the only thing the attendees' had in common. The lack of diversity amongst guest stood out like a sore thumb. Typically a Woman's wedding is one of the most, if not the most exciting and monumental days in her life. Still, not one of Jalisa's blood relatives was in attendance. Sadly the only brown faces seen were of she and her off springs. If a person just so happened to walk up they wouldn't be too sure if they were attending a wedding or a Donald Trump Rally.

However, choosing to look at the bright side, this might have been a good thing, there's no telling what would have occured if the two sides would have been too close. Mite have turned into world war 3.

The fact that none of her relatives made an appearance really wasn't too much of a surprise. Despite the fact that they too had used and abused her throughout her life, once they all caught wind of Tim's treatment, everyone all of a sudden grew a heart and demanded that she not only leave Tim, but cut all ties.

Once she refused, she was disowned. This only made Jalisa even more dependent on him, now knowing without a shadow of a doubt that without him, she would be forced to fend for herself in the cold world.

Nevertheless she held on to the thought that the now official Union of she and Tim would somehow cast her into being a full blown citizen of the white race she still was in dire need to be accepted by. This was only wishful thinking. To every one of Tim's family members she was still Tim's 'Black Bitch' nothing more, nothing less. Not saying they didn't like her. It just was what it was. Even Tim's kids were looked upon as outsiders. No one ever really said it to their faces though. Tim was still known as a Bad Motherfucker but something's just go without saying.

Can't forget to menton the fact thatArieus wasn't one of Tim's kid. He on the other hand was treated like dirt, actually worse than dirt, scum, like some shit that you look at that instantly disgust you. Like something that just makes you mad at the mere mention of it.

You'd think Jalisa would at least put forth an effort to stop the mistreatment. No, she was too busy trying to stay on Tim's good side to ever give a fuck about what was going on with Arieus. Well maybe that's not all the way true. Can't say for sure she didn't give a fuck, it's more like she didn't know what to do. Most parents put their kids first. Apparently Jalisa wasn't strong enough for that. During the entire Wedding Ceremony she acted as if her only boy was nonexistent. As his entire immediate family stood in front of a large Confederate Flag, prepared for pictures, he sat alone staring off into the world.

"Are you apart of the family?" asked the photographer, to Arieus, after double taking, discovering that he had an undeniable resemblance to Jalisa.

Tim overhears him. "That aint my fucking family. Mind your business and take the damn picture," he says as he points his finger toward the photographer.

"Calm down Timmy," blurted Tim's mother who was standing next to the photographer, barefoot, clutching a beer can. "Leave the nice picture man alone. He didn't know."

Like always Jalisa drops her head in attempt to act as though she's oblivious to the things that are going on around her. At the same time every other eye in attendance had turned over to Arieus. Of course this makes him noticeably nervous, sweating pirfusely, desperately wishing something or someone would come along to redirect everyone's focus.

"Mom, Shut up," Tim shouts. "Everybody just needs to mind their damn business. His little black ass can find his Dad if he wants a fucking family picture," he finishes before looking over to the photographer, placing his beer behind him. "Now take the damn picture."

"1, 2, 3, Smile," the poise photographer screams as everyone holds their position.

It's funny what the power that something as simple as a camera possesses. Upon taking a glance at the picture, one could assume that they were one big happy family. Teeth on display, heads high, eyes bright, no one would ever guess the pain and dysfunction that truly existed within them.

Later on, in the wee hours of the morning, like a madman Tim whips up into the driveway of their new family home. The back of his truck reads 'Just Married'. He still sports his tuxedo from earlier, only now he's seemed to have misplaced a couple accessories, including his right shoe and a few buttons from his collared shirt.

He thrusts open the driver side door, stumbling out, pissy drunk, trying with all of his mite to make it up the porch steps. After falling to the ground at least 5 times and almost falling even more, he finally makes it to the front door where he blindly searches for the key whole. Over and over he attempts to slide it in, nearly giving up until finally accomplishing his goal before barging into his home where he's instantly met by Jalisa, standing by the far end of the living room at the entrance of the kitchen.

"You Bitch," she screams as tears stream down her face.

"What did I do baby?" Tim mutters drunkenly before ducking for cover. Jalisa clearly had enough, resulting in her launching a glass dead in Tim's direction. "What the fuck," he yells.

"You lucky Motherfucker," she screams, upset at the fact that she'd missed her target. Not giving up on her rampage, she rushes over to Tim in full attack mode.

"Oh shit," Tim yells as Jalisa pounces onto him, scratching and screaming. "Get the fuck off me you crazy bitch," Tim yells before using all of his strength, finally forcing her off of him. Only for her to rush back into the kitchen.

"Our fucking Wedding night," she continues to scream.

"Ahh shut up," Tim mumbles still stumbling, checking his body for blood before looking up only to discover that Jalisa had now gathered a gang of plates and was preparing to sling them like Frisbee's in his direction.

"Ima be right back Jalisa, I'm going to the store," she says as she mocks him, launching the first plate.

"Calm down," Tim bolts as he stumbles towards the kitchen, miraculously dodging plate after plate as glass scatters throughout the room.

Still not giving up, Jalisa now decides to go for the butcher knife. She's never acted in this manner before, it was as if she was possessed. Or maybe all of her bottled up emotions had finally took a toll on her.

On second thought she was probably just doing what most women in her positon would do if their Husband committed such an act on their Wedding Night. Like, who would do such a thing? Tim Anderson, that's who.

As the two meet up, Tim attempts to grab the knife, only he was too slow. By the time he could realize what was going on Jalisa had already managed to have the knife pressed up against his throat, causing his body to suddenly tense up as he through both hands up in the air, standing stiff as a statue, thinking of an escape plan. "Baby put the knife down," he says calmly.

Jalisa remains silent for a second as tears continue to flood her face. "It's two in the morning. I been waiting for you all fucking night. I don't deserve this shit, I don't deserve it."

Tim timidly speaks, "You're right baby. I'm wrong. I know I'm wrong I just had a little business to handle that's all."

"Business? Motherfucker do I look like I was born yesterday. Aint no fucking business."

"Baby, baby, baby, let me explain," Tim pleads, shaking.

"Don't explain shit bitch. I got half a mind to pack all my shit and take them kids right now," she says staring evilly into Tim's eyes.

Big mistake. While she figured she had Tim right where she wanted, he had found his escape. Knowing that she was busy locking eyes with him, he took the chance at violently grabbing the knife. It worked. Wasting no time, he twisted Jalisa's wrist until finally she released the knife before slowly dropping to the ground in pain.

"Tim stop it. You're hurting me." Jalisa whined.

"Take my kids?" Tim asks as his hand remains wrapped around Jalisa's tiny wrist. Bending down to the floor along with her he asks, "Bitch is that what you said? Huh? Huh? Where you gonna go. Huh? You gonna go to your crackhead Mom who didn't even come to your own fucking wedding. Huh? Huh? You gonna get you a nigger boyfriend so he can fuck you and leave you. Huh? Or maybe one that will Pimp you out like your Daddy. Huh? Huh? Is that what you're gonna do? Huh?"

"Tim stop you're hurting me."

"Fuck you going. Huh? Tell me bitch," Tim shouts.

"Tim stop it."

"Don't ever say you're taking my kids from me. You and that little ugly nigger son of yours can go anytime you please," said Tim as chunks of saliva shoot out of his mouth as he spoke. "But if you ever, and I mean ever threaten to take my kids again it'll be the last time your black ass'll ever threaten anybody or anything again in your motherfucking life. You hear me bitch?"

"Yes Tim," says Jalisa, in obvious pain.

"Huh? I can't hear you. I said do you fucking hear me bitch?" Tim, asks as he tightens his grip.

"Yes Tim," shouts Jalisa.

Tossing her arm, Tim stands to his feet as Jalisa's exhausted body plummeted to the floor. Stepping over her, slightly kicking her in the process, he ignores her screams as if she were a stranger.

"I'm going to bed," Tim says.

On route to the bedroom he passes the room in which the kids slept. It's a decent sized room. Faith and Grace both sleep on bunkbeds, Amanda has a small twin sized bed to herself on the opposite side of the room, while Arieus sleeps in the corner next to the closet along with an old couch pillow and sheet from the Trailer Park days.

Despite being the least comfortable of the bunch, Arieus still manages sleep peacefully, unaffected by his Mothers Pain. The girls on the other hand took a more humane approach, each one sobbing gently into their pillows, longing for relief from their all too often pain.

Morning time. The house is lit up as the sun beams through the cracks in the blinds. Still, Arieus doesn't need that to awaken him this morning.

"**AHHHHHHHH**," he screams springing from the floor kicking, screaming and crying, awakening the entire room.

"Not again," Amanda whines. "Mom Arieus pissed himself again," she screams to the other room.

Arieus looks down at his crotch, wet yet again. He drops his head. He's gone through this enough to know this was bad. Real bad.

Faith looks over to him. "Eww, you stink."

After only falling asleep a few minutes prior, Jalisa trots into the room eyes half shut. "Come on Arieus. You're eight years old. You can't keep pissing yourself every time you have a bad dream."

Arieus says "Sorry" in a voice so low it's almost impossible to comprehend.

"Ok. Just get up and clean yourself off. It's almost time for school anyway. I'll clean up the sheets. Bring them to me."

Standing up, Arieus grabs the sheets and walks towards the door when out of the darkness his worst enemy, the Devil in the flesh,

Tim appears. Belt in hand, eyes cocked, focused as Arieus unintentionally gasps, dropping the sheets to the floor.

"You pissing yourself again boy?" Tim asks in a dark whisper.

Like he and his Mother seem too often do, Arieus drops his head.

"Huh? Huh? You pissing your fucking self?" asks Tim. "You know the routine. Strip," Tim shouts.

Without a sound Arieus slowly begins to remove his undershirt.

"Boy, I aint got all damn day," Tim blurts before cocking back smacking Arieus on the leg with the leather belt. "Hurry up," he says as Arieus drops his underwear while his siblings and Mother stand around watching.

No more than a couple seconds after Arieus's underwear hit the dirty carpet Tim had Arieus's right arm raised in the air fiercely slapping the belt against his adolescent frame as he screamed in agonizing pain. This only made things worse. Fuel to the fire. Arieus had yet to discover that crying was like strapping an extra battery to Tim's back. His smile widened with every whipping.

"I was kind enough to let you sleep on that floor in the same room as my daughters. You wanna sleep on the porch? Huh? Huh?" Tim spoke before throwing Arieus to the ground. Staring a piercing whole through him, he states, "You black dirty motherfucker. I hate you," he said looking down at Arieus's urine soaked underwear. "Put them damn draws back on. Your little black ass is going to school just like that. You wanna make my house smell like piss than you're gonna go to school smelling like it. See how you like that, nigger," Tim says before walking away.

Arieus and Amanda are the last kids to walk onto a crowded school bus. There's a mixture of kids. Blacks, whites and Asian, mostly black though.

As always Amanda has no problem finding a seat as she links up with her young white friend, Ashley Perry. Even though Amanda never had the latest clothes or shoes, her gorgeous high yellow face made up for it. Ultimately allowing her to grow to be one of the most popular girls in school. Together she and Ashley, whose parents were rich compared to Amanda, gave off a vibe that they thought they were better than you.

"Hey Amanda," says Ashley.

"Hey Ashley," Amanda follows with a smile.

"I love your shoes," adds Ashley.

"Thanks," she says looking down at her Wal-Mart baby doll shoes. There was nothing special about them at all but sometimes when you're super popular whatever you do is cool.

While they small talked Arieus stood in the aisle searching for an available seat. As he scans the bus, heads shake from left to right. This isn't anything abnormal for him. Sadly it's an everyday occurrence.

"Ay boy," Ms. Johnson, the overweight bus driver screams back to Arieus, looking at him through the rearview mirror. "Hurry up and find a seat. I'm getting sick and tired of telling you this every day," she says as she pulls off.

At this same time a kid sitting in the back of the bus launches a balled up sheet of paper towards him, knocking him in the head. Of course all the kids laugh and point. Arieus had grown immune though. He took it in stride. Unfazed he remained focused on his quest for an empty seat.

Then Bam! He spots one directly in front of Ashley and Amanda. Knowing he still smelled of sour piss, he thought long and hard on just what to do. If he sat there than Ashley would know for sure that he's stinky and that could result in Amanda getting mad. And when Amanda's mad, who knows what that could mean. After all she held the power to tell Tim and the porch could end up his permanent bedroom.

Unable to think of any other options, the siblings make eye contact and with her eyes Amanda assures Arieus that his thoughts were indeed true.

"Didn't I say have a seat already," repeats Ms. Johnson.

Out of options, still staring at Amanda, he's forced to make a decision he was sure he'd regret, closing his eyes Arieus slowly slid his way over to the open spot, gently easing his way into the seat, he was quite aware that flopping down could cause the odor to mistakenly fly out uncontrollably, smacking everyone in the nose.

Still it didn't matter. His stench was far too strong. Dontrell, a natural loudmouth sitting in front of Arieus turns around with his face screwed up. "Hey what's that smell? Did you piss on yourself?"

Amanda grows red with embarrassment.

"Yo you stink," he says looking around to assure he had the entire busses attention. "You need a diaper little baby?"

In an instant nearly every kid on the bus all pointed, laughing at Arieus before Mike Ross, a chubby black kid sitting in the back of the bus shouts out, "Arieus the Smelliest."

Like a chain reaction everyone follows suit. "Arieus the Smelliest. Arieus the Smelliest."

Any normal kid would have probably cried their little heart out. But not Arieus. Accustom to the ways of the cruel world. He plays it cool, staring out the window emotionless.

Amanda on the other hand, wasn't nearly as strong. Fighting back tears of anger, she thought to herself, why out of all the brothers in the world, God had to curse her with 'Arieus the Smelliest'?

"Hold on, hold on bruh," says Pete as he sits on his bottom bunk. "What the fuck is up with you and this peeing in the bed shit? You got some type of disorder or something?" asks Pete.

"I don't know," replies Arieus still staring at the ceiling.

"You don't know? Well nigga don't you think you need to find out? You a grown ass man still pissing on himself. That shit aint normal. Is you having bad dreams or something? Like what the fuck is going on? I'm sorry man but I need some answers. That shit is beyond crazy. Not to mention, your shit is foul. You stunk up the whole cell the other day. You might need to start drinking more water bruh."

"All my life I've always had these crazy ass nightmares where I was about to die and right before I died. I'd wake up screaming at the top of my lungs. And it never fails. I'd always piss my pants. Just can't help it. Doesn't matter what I drink, eat, nothing, It just happens."

"Damn. And that bitch ass nigga Tim beat your ass every time?"

"Not every time. Sometimes he was too drunk to even notice."

"Damn. That's crazy," Pete says shaking his head. "He had you all naked in front of your sisters and shit. That shit is sick. I seen my Pops get smoked in front of my face when I was a kid but you making me feel as if that shit wont nothing compared to shit you was going through."

"Hey. It's life."

"That's crazy though. Dog, your life really was fucked up. I don't know what the hell I would've done. Especially seeing how school was just as worse as home. Knowing me, my little ass would've probably dropped out. Fuck it," Pete speaks before laying down on his rack. "Aint like whatever Tim or your Mom did about it was going to be any worse than what the fuck was already going on."

"Yeah, school was bad," Arieus agrees. "But I saw things a little differently than you see them. From my perspective back then, school was the best place for me to be. I had a real fascination with the teachers. Other kids wanted to be Dr.'s, lawyers and Football players. I instead wanted to be one of them."

"A fucking teacher? Man fuck that. I hated school. Real talk, one of the only perks about being in Prison is that my ass aint got to go to school. I swear every year around August and September I thank God that I aint gotta get up and go there. Aint nothing in the world would've ever made me want to be a damn teacher."

"Wow. I've never heard anyone say they hated school that much."

"Well now you have. Back then I looked at teachers in the same light as the Police. Well until I met this nigga name Mr. Johnson. He was a good nigga. Shit, still is, he's part of the reason I'm even getting an appeal now. He treat a nigga just like a son. But still that shit aint never make me wanna be a teacher. I can tell you was way different than me though. You look like one of them smart ass niggas. I bet you made straight A's, didn't you?

"Basically. School work took me to another world. I felt like I needed it. I can't say I loved sitting in a boring class all day listening to teachers but I was on the pursuit of happiness. And I just looked at it as a pit stop along the way."

"Huh?"

"Teachers always talked about how we needed school so we could get into a good college. And there were colleges all around the world."

"Oh, ok. I get it," Pete says as he nods. "So college was your escape plan."

"Exactly. College represented a brand new life. I could start over. I wanted friends. I wanted people who loved me but it was clear I was never gonna get that without getting away."

"Damn bruh. Ok so let me ask you this. Did you ever in any moment have any good times at the crib?"

"Yeah. Being alone."

"Alone? I been locked up in solitude too damn much too ever appreciate being alone. How the hell is that fun?"

"When I was about five or six I created something like my own world. In reality I had nothing that I wanted. But in this world I could just lay back and have entire control over a whole universe. It was my dreamland. I know you're going to judge me but growing up I never had any toys of my own so I'd always sneak off and play with Amanda's Dolls," Arieus confessed. "In my head the dolls were my family. And the Ken doll was my Dad."

"The Ken Doll was your Dad? Ok. I aint gon judge you. But I can't lie that shit does sound weird as hell."

"Well as you should already be able to tell. I was weird. Still am. I can remember hating when Amanda would come and play with them. Controlling them was the closest I could get to being God.I loved my dreamland."

"God? Damn. I can't even lie. It sound like your little dreamland was a good ass place to be," Pete says, in admiration.

"Yeah it was. Until it was time to wake back up to reality."

2000

Faith and Grace sit in the living room, laid up on the family's plastic covered couch inside their latest home. It's not a mansion but it's sure as hell a lot bigger than their last two bedroom shack. Like their previous homes the carpet is littered with trash, clothes and old stains. However the family did take the time to place pictures alongside their walls. In total there were about 10 and of course not one had poor Arieus in it.

As Faith and Grace, who have grown to be gorgeous young ladies, occupy their time, watching cartoons, Jalisa prepares diner a few feet behind them in the kitchen. Pretty sure you've already guessed, it's a mess. Dishes piled up to the ceiling, while splatters of food rest spreaded out across the walls. Judging from the looks of things, one might quickly decide to opt out of receiving something as simple as a glass of water, let alone a meal from inside. That's only until the aroma of Jalisa's spinach Lasagna attacks your nose. She might not have learned too many valuable lessons from her family but cooking sure was one of them.

With usually no television to watch or radio to listen to Jalisa spent many of her adolescent days watching her Grandmother whip up everything from Collard Greens, to Pig feet, never once serving anything less than delicious.

70

Like her Grandmother, cooking took Jalisa's mind off the harsh realities of her day to day life. She'd cut that stove on, turn up the radio and zone out, entering her own little world where she made the rules.

"Joy and Pain..Sunshine and Rain," Jalisa sings along with the music, still managing to keep her cigarette dangling from her dark lips. Over the years, between the stress of dealing with Tim and raising kids, along with her addiction to cigarettes and beer, she'd grown to lose her girlish looks. She wasn't an ugly woman by a long shot but the trials and tribulations of life were definitely written in cursive all over her face. As she removed the cigarette from her lips to take a gulp from her oversized glass of Steel Reserve, she opens her cabinet, only to realize she's missing salt, a key ingredient for her meal. "Shit," she blurts as she walks over to the living room.

"Mom, I'm starving. When's the food gonna be ready?" asks Grace.

"In a minute," answers Jalisa.

"Who starts cooking dinner at 10 at night?" adds Faith, full of attitude as usual.

"You know I can make it so that you don't eat at all," barks Jalisa, sternly, looking over to Faith. "You wanna eat so bad fix it your damn self," she adds pointing to the kitchen. "Tired of you ungrateful ass kids," she says as she takes another drag from her cigarette.

Mumbling to herself Jalisa walks past Amanda's room where she sits on her full sized bed changing a crying, Cameron. The newest addition to the family. After years of effort, Tim had finally gotten his precious baby boy.

Jalisa smiles as she glances inside of the room. "Aw it's gonna be ok baby," she says before continuing to walk further down the hall.

She stops and knocks on the closed door of Arieus's room. The now 15 year old lays on the twin sized bed of his closet sized room staring up at the ceiling. His acne riddled face matches the bumpy tiles. He sits up, "Come in," he says as his meditation session is interrupted.

Jalisa opens the door. "Arieus I need you to walk to the store and pick up me some salt."

"Ok."

"Thanks," she says closing the door as Arieus stands tall to his feet. At only 15 he was already 6'2, it's safe to say he inherited his height from his biological father considering Jalisa was a fairly short lady.

This too angered Tim, at only 5'7 he hated the fact that Arieus had grown to be bigger than he was. Deep down he knew that it was quite possible for Arieus to get the best of him in a fist fight. Still, that didn't stop his antics. Actually it made him worse, causing him to instill ultimate fear, ensuring that Arieus would never even entertain the thought to even look to him in the wrong manner.

As Arieus dresses to go on his mission, a few blocks down, the pinky finger of Aban Shabazz, a middle aged Arabian man is gently pressing a red emergency button beneath the counter of his convenience store, 'The Brother's' as Big Stick, a stocky black man draped in all black with a matching bandana over his face, holds a chrome 9 millimeter handgun to Aban's head.

Aban's blood boils as he reaches into the register, forking over all of his hard earned cash into a black bag Big Stick had handed him moments earlier. It's taking everything in him not to attempt to knock the pistol out of Big Stick's hand. Knowing that he's the family's sole bread winner, he remains calm. Thinking to himself how this Nigger thug would never try such a stunt like this back home in his native county, Pakistan. In fact, he wouldn't make it a day.

However he is thankful that his 12 year old daughter Adiba and 10 year old son Ali were sick with the flu. Any other day they'd be right by his side.

"Man hurry the fuck up before I smoke your motherfuckin ass. Goddamn." yells Stick.

"I'm going as fast as I can," says Aban in an Arabian accent.

"Fuck that. Nigga, hurry the fuck up like I said. I don't give a fuck about none of that shit you talking, I'll smoke your motherfucking ass. Fuck wrong with you. Foreign ass bitch, hurry the fuck up like I said."

Aban clenches his teeth tightly struggling to keep his composure as he hands the bag over to Stick.

Before latching on, Stick remembers he'd just ran out of Newport Cigarettes. At home he had a fifth of Hennessey on the rocks and he'd just popped a gram of Molly. There was no way he could have the two without a pack of blows. Where he was from, Henny, Molly, and Newport's go together like sausage, eggs, and grits. Sure you could have one without the other but come on, who wants to live like that?

"Ay my nigga. Throw some Newport's in that bitch," demands Stick.

"Ok," replies Aban.

"Hurry up. Damn," he says looking around nervously.

Aban throws a box into the bag.

"More motherfucker. Hell wrong with you?" he shouts.

Aban, takes a breath as he throws about five more boxes into the bag.

"Alright, alright. That's enough," Stick yells at he snatches the bag. "I'm out."

Darting out of the store he holds on to the waist of his sagging jeans as he heads to the side of the building where he'd parked his car, throws the key into the ignition, only to be disappointed. Nothing happens, not a sound. The car was dead as a door knob.

Losing his cool, he looks out the front window, making sure no Police were in route. Seeing none, he looks down at the gas tank. It's full. "What the fuck," he screams, panicking, smacking the steering wheel. After cranking it once more to no avail it finally dawns on him. The fucking gas gauge was broken. His cousin Dumbass Dan had told him about it the other day but he was busy playing PlayStation so he really wasn't listening. It was 4th quarter and he was down two in NBA Live 2000, so naturally it went in one ear and out the other. At that moment it all came back like a boomerang to him. Too bad it was too late. "Fuck," he shouts as he throws the car keys to the dash board.

Unaware of the fact that Aban had pressed the emergency button his hearts drops into his stomach as he suddenly discovers the glare of police lights ahead of him. "Oh shit," he scarcely says to himself. Without any other option. He grabs his bag and gun before fleeing on foot in the opposite direction of the Police lights.

Instantly the two police units spot him and commence to chasing him down on hot pursuit as he dashes down the street,

75

running for his life. Not figuratively, literally, he was on probation for a past armed robbery. One more offense would definitely send him away for life. Especially since this time around he would have no one to snitch on.

While Stick hits his 40 yard dash, Arieus is casually walking towards him, on his way to the same store Stick had just robbed, head down, oblivious to what's going on. He can hear the sirens but has no idea Stick is about to collide with him as he bulldozes his way down the street.

"What in the world," screams Arieus as the two violently meet, both men being knocked to the ground.

"What the fuck? Fuck out my way little nigga." shouts Stick as he pushes Arieus off of him and keeps trucking.

Brushing himself off, Arieus quickly stands to his feet, trying to make sense of what the hell had just occurred, only to be briefly blinded by the lights of the two Police vehicles who nearly run over the side walk as they suddenly turn the corner.

Still in shock he looks down as his eyes bulge from his head. "Wow," he says to himself, staring mesmerized at Sticks gun, a chrome .22 laying flat on the ground. He'd dropped it but with all of the commotion, he'd failed to notice.

After snapping back into reality, Arieus takes a look around before carefully reaching down to pick up his latest possession, examining it from an up close and personal perspective. He smiled as his heart raced. Not only was this his first time holding a gun, it was also his first time actually seeing one. It was love at first site.

Regaining focus on the reason for his travels, he tucks the gun into his side, covering it with his coat. Strutting to the store, he now possessed a more confident stroll, head to the sky. That night would have definitely been the wrong night for anybody to crack one of those 'Arieus the Smelliest' jokes.

After about 35 minutes he finally returns home. It would have been quicker but Aban closed shop due to Big Stick's dumbass and Arieus was forced to travel 5 more blocks down the street to another store. Not to mention, he took his time as he stepped, he wanted to spend as much alone time with his new best friend as possible.

"Finally," says Grace as Arieus stepped into the house.

"Oh my God, I thought you were Dad," whines Amanda as she walks into the living room carrying Cameron. Her and Arieus both walk towards the kitchen where Arieus hands Jalisa the groceries before walking out, leaving Amanda and Jalisa alone. "Mom where's Dad? I got a huge test tomorrow and I left my back pack at Paula's and I need a ride over to get it."

"I don't know. I guess he had to work late. Call him," Jalisa says, opening the grocery bag, retrieving the salt.

"Wow. I never thought of that," says Amanda, sarcastically. "I've been calling him for hours. He won't answer, he's been off work since three."

"Well shit, I don't know where the fuck he is," says Jalisa as she puts the finishing touches on diner.

"Oh my God. How don't you know where your own husband is? I swear this has to be the worst fucking family ever," says Amanda before storming back to her room.

"Hey Bitch! You better watch your Motherfucking mouth," screams Jalisa.

"How longs it gonna take now?" screams Grace, to the kitchen.

"Hold the fuck on. Shit, I'ma let you know. I swear I wish I never had y'all little worrisome motherfuckers," she says taking a sip from her bottle. "How about somebody do something for me for a Goddamn change. Fuck," she yells.

As the night progresses the mood lightens. Kids eats. Still no Tim. More dishes pile up. Still no Tim. Roaches eat. Still no Tim. Everyone bathes and prepare for the next day. Still no Tim. Finally everyone falls asleep. Still no fucking Tim. Unsurprisingly no one hears anything regarding him until about 3:00 a.m.

"Hello," speaks Jalisa into her house phone from the side of the bed as she wipes the cole out of her eyes. "Yes this is she," she says before pausing. "Oh my God," she screams awakening the entire house.

See, Tim had been off of work for hours. But as usual he was out having the time of his life with his favorite mistress, the vivacious, Linda. Tall, Brunette, tits that sat up like a soldier and an hour glass frame to match.

Everything was all good as they staggered their way out of Tim's favorite hangout, 'The Blue Buggy Bar' around 1:30 a.m., drunk as hell, kissing and groping one another in such a manner that no one in their right mind would ever mistake Tim for a married man. If so then he obviously had to be married to Linda. After all what kind of fool would participate in such acts when anyone in the city could ride past to witness. But like always, Tim Anderson, that's who.

"Baby can I drive your car?" asked Linda as they finally arrived at Tim's Truck.

"Drive my car? Baby are you crazy? You're drunk," Tim replies grinning, holding on to the door handle in order to keep his balance.

"Yeah but baby you're drunk too," she follows, clutching Tim's waist as they stood face to face.

"You're right," said Tim, bursting out into a drunken laughter.

79

"So I can drive? Please?" she asked as she rubbed her right hand ever so gently onto his rising penis.

"Ok," he says as he clumsily reaches into his pockets. "But you be careful. This is my baby," he said before handing over the keys. The same keys that he never even let Jalisa come within 10 feet of.

"Don't worry baby. I've been driving since I was 12 and drinking since I was 8," she says before grabbing Tim by the collar pulling him in for a long sultry kiss. "You have nothing to worry about, sweet stuff."

"I fucking love you," Tim states.

"And I love you more Big Papa," she follows before opening the driver's side door flopping inside as Tim did the same on the passenger side.

"I can't wait to get you home," said Tim looking over to her.

"And why is that?" asked Linda as she failed to put the key into the ignition for the third time.

"You'll see," Tim's says flirtatiously.

"Oooh I can't wait," she says as she finally gets the key into the hole. "I love surprises," she says as she sped off smiling from ear to ear.

That smile wouldn't last long. Approximately a minute later after Tim had somehow dozed off into a drunken stuper, Linda sped through a red light colliding head on with another vehicle.

Thursday (cont..)

"Damn," says Pete, laying down.

"Yep. Linda died. Unfortunately Tim didn't. Got fucked up pretty badly though. He stayed in the hospital for 33 days. Best 33 days of my life."

"Shit nigga. I bet. You make me actually appreciate not having a man around growing up," Pete says shaking his head. "How did the rest of your fam feel about that?"

"Honestly no one really gave a damn about Tim. Truthfully we were happy to be getting a vacation. Actually, for the first time in me and my sibling's life's we finally had something in common."

"What about your Mom? She was happy too?" asks Pete as he stands up, walking over to the metal toilet a few feet away from his rack.

"She talked like she was hurt but I could tell she was happy. And she was even happier that Linda was out of the picture."

"Oh shit," says Pete as he urinates into the toilet. "So she knew about Linda the whole time?"

"Yep. Linda wasn't a secret and neither was Mary, Beth, Vicki, and the rest of them."

82

"Damn boy. That's crazy," says Pete as he uses his foot to flush the toilet.

"Yeah. Me and my fam still didn't talk but I went from being treated like an inmate to being treated like I was invisible," says Arieus as Pete turns around to talk to him face to face.

"Huh? What the fuck is the difference. Who in the hell wants to be treated like their invisible. That shit don't sound good at all to me."

"Trust me, it was. Just put yourself in my position," Arieus speaks, finally turning to Pete. "When I was seen, I felt as though I pissed everyone off just from the mere look at me. Being invisible was amazing. I could walk through the house freely, without worrying about anybody talking any shit to me. It was like a new world I was living in. It was the best feeling I'd ever had and I was determined to keep it for as long as I could."

"Hold on before you start telling the story again. I gotta ask about the gun."

"I'm getting to that. Just be patient."

It was finally time for Tim to return to his castle and like any good wife would do, Jalisa went all out. Yeah she might've partially enjoyed her time away from her abusive husband but she'd hoped that the accident would somehow give him a new lease on life. Maybe make him appreciate what was in front of him.

Excited, she threw on her best clothes, squirted a dab of Tim's favorite perfume 'Exclamation', got a fresh perm, painted her toes and finger nails, shaved her pussy and went to get her man.

After retrieving him, making no pit stops, they pulled up into the driveway. Although Tim slept the entire ride she still believed in her heart that things were about to be different. Snoring as usual, Jalisa nudges his shoulder, awakening him before getting out of the car, opening the back door, pulling out Tim's crutches and walking over to the passenger side to assist him.

"Hey Dad," shouted, Amanda, Faith and Grace from the porch. They too were excited, hoping their Dad had learned a thing or two since his near death experience.

"Whatsup," says Tim, failing to even so much as look up to them as he spoke.

During his stay in the hospital he'd requested for them not to visit. He said he didn't want anyone to see him in his condition. For that to be his reaction after not seeing his family for over a month was pretty heartbreaking for the kids. Luckily over the years they'd grown nearly numb to his cold ways.

As his family dysfuntionally reunites, Arieus peeked through the blinds of his room, emotionless, he watched as Tim hopped his way to the porch and up the steps. "You guys don't have to keep touching me. I got this. I'm not no fucking cripple," he strongly stated as Faith held open the screen door for him while the rest of the girls backed off. "What the fuck," he shouts as he enters the home.

Everyone timidly looks to Tim as they walk in behind him.

"What Baby?" asks Jalisa.

"This house is a fucking mess. Did you guys have a party while I was gone?" he asks before looking over to Jalisa, with a bulldog's snarl. "I gotta do everything around here? Are you not smart enough to give the kids some fucking chores," he says pointing at the few out of place items placed throughout the house.

In all honesty, the crib actually looked far better than it had ever did when he was home. The floor was vacuumed, dishes washed, windows sprayed down, even the wood works had been scrubbed by Arieus and Jalisa herself. Dude was tripping, no map.

Looking up to the girls, he continues his complaints, "Am I raising little girls or fucking men. What the fuck? This is what I come home to? Really," he says disgusted, as the girls all look away in different directions?

"We tried our best but everyone was a little bu--" attempts Jalisa, trying to explain before being cut off.

"I don't wanna hear that shit. I'm going to my fucking room. I don't have time for the bullshit."

Jalisa slowly walks Tim to the bedroom, cautiously guiding him, unsure of exactly how much, if any help he desired. Feeling drained, she takes a look back at her devastated daughters standing behind her. Each one with the same helpless look in their eyes.

Meanwhile Arieus lays in bed staring at the ceiling. He can hear Tim and his Mom as they speak.

"Sit me down gently, sit me down gently. Whew," he says as Jalisa eases him onto their Queen sized bed. "Shit. We gotta get a new bed. The hospital bed was better than this crap."

"I was just thinking the same thing," agrees Jalisa. "Oh yeah me and the girls cooked your favorite diner," she adds with a smile.

"I'm not hungry," replies Tim as he lays back onto the bed.

"Oh. Ok. Well it'll be ready whenever you are."

"Just get me a beer," he says as he stretches his neck, scanning the room for other things to possibly gripe about.

"Ok," says Jalisa as she searches for her purse.

"What the hell are you doing?" Tim asks, vexed, looking over to her.

"Looking for my purse I swear I just had i--."

"Getting your purse?" Tim interrupts.

"Yeah I'm about to go to the store for you," replies Jalisa, unsure of where Tim's attitude was stemming from.

"Why the fuck didn't you have some fucking beers for me when I came home? What the fuck is wrong with you?"

"I didn't know if you were still going to be drinking after the accident."

"Huh? What the fuck is wrong with you?" Tim shouts. "I swear you're the dumbest bitch I've ever met," he adds.

A tear drops falls from Jalisa's face as she finally discovers her purse hanging from the closet doorknob. She walks over to retrieve it as Tim lays back shaking his head in disappointment.

Upon returning from the store, for the remainder of the night things continued to go right back to the hell they were all used to before Tim's departure. Something about his presence made everyone stiff, even the lights seemed to darken. Master Tim was back on the Plantation and he was in full effect.

After walking on eggshells the entire night the next morning is no different as everyone tips toes around determined not to awake the beast as Tim lays peaceful in another drunken sleep. He'd popped an excess of pain meds and had passed out around 8 and hadn't so much as blinked since. Turns out Jalisa had shaved her kitty for nothing.

Soon the uncomfortable silence had gone on far too long for baby Cameron, he'd had enough. Out of nowhere he began yelling and crying uncontrollably. Amanda tried to tame him but he just wasn't having it. Maybe he somehow knew that his own Dad hadn't even asked about him once since he'd been home and was trying to make his presence felt. Who knows, but his behavior seemed to be contagious as Jalisa found herself also forgetting that her husband lay asleep. "Faith, Grace! Your bus is outside," she screamed as she buttoned up her stained McDonald's shirt.

"I can't find my blue ribbon." says Faith, walking out into the living room as Jalisa signals with her index finger over her mouth to quiet down.

"Ay shut that shit up. I'm trying to get some fucking sleep here. Shit," Tim screamed from the bedroom.

"See what you did," Jalisa whispered. "Fuck that blue Ribbon. Your bus is waiting," she continues, pointing outside.

"I can't go to school looking like this," replies Faith, quietly.

"You got 10 seconds to get out of this house. You aint going to school for no damn fashion show," says Jalisa, low and stern.

Arieus emerges from his room dressed in gear no black teen in their right mind would dare be caught dead in; Nascar tee, lee, straight fit jeans and Shaq shoes, all from Wal-Mart. On a scale from 1-10 his dressing game was on negative 50. By now though, he'd been teased so much that the students didn't even really pay him that much attention anymore. Not to say they never had a few jokes here and there but nothing too bad. He was pretty much old news.

As Arieus walks to the exit, Grace also trots out of her room toward the front door. She along with her twin sister's clothing weren't the trendiest but they were nowhere near as outdated as Arieus's.

"Oh my God! I can't believe you're making me go to school looking like this," says Faith, studying herself in the mirror. She sported pigtails with a white ribbon on the left, but nothing on the right.

"Didn't I say get out," replies Jalisa as she pushes Faith and Grace out of the front door as Arieus follows behind.

As they depart Amanda walks into the living room holding Cameron, who still has of yet to stop crying. "What's wrong

Cammy?" Jalisa whispers in a baby's voice as she combs her hair in the same mirror Faith had been looking into.

"Nothing at all. He's just in a crying mood today," says Amanda. She'd been working at the local McDonalds along with Jalisa so she was fly, hair laid, draped in Roca Wear, with fresh air force ones to match.

"Ay shut that damn baby up," screams Tim once again.

"Just take him outside for a second," says Jalisa as Cameron seemed to be purposely pissing Tim off, screaming louder than before. "I'm going to go check on your Dad."

"Ok," Amanda says rolling her eyes as Jalisa makes her way to her bedroom.

"You sure you're gonna be alright being home alone all day?" asks Jalisa as she stepped into her bedroom. To herself, she prayed Tim didn't snap.

He nods, never lifting his eyelids.

"Well there's a plate in the fridge if you get hungry," she follows as she grabs her purse and walks towards the door. "Bye Baby."

Tim grunts as Jalisa exits the room. She's thankful, knowing things could have been far worse.

"Mom come get Cam. My rides out here," whispers Amanda from outside, cracking the screen door open.

"Ok just go put him in his carseat," she whispers back as she walks from the kitchen. "I'll get his baby bag," she says as she grabs it up from off of the couch before walking out the front door.

Mike Ross, the same kid who started the infamous 'Arieus the Smelliest' had grown out of his chubby stage and was now Amanda's boyfriend. He sits awaiting her in an old beat down Honda Accord. Not that the condition of his car mattered. To High Schoolers in Norfolk, this was top of the line. After all, anything was better than walking and by this time Amanda was way too fine to be beating her feet. At 17 she was a splitting image of her mother at that age, only a lighter complexed version, to Mike and basically any other boy she came across, she was a prize.

"You ready for day care Cammi?" says Amanda as she buckles Cam into his seat belt.

"Thanks girl," Jalisa says to Amanda as she walks up. "Oh I see you stopped all that crazy crying," she says looking at baby Cameron as he smiled, showcasing his deep dimples.

"Yeah. I guess he wasn't feeling the vibe in the house," says Amanda. "But anyway I'll see you later."

"Ok. Bye Amanda. "

"Bye Mom. Bye Cameron," Amanda says as she hops in the front seat of Mike's whip.

"How you doing Mrs. Anderson?" asks Mike, waving over to Jalisa.

"I'm good. Hey Mike," Jalisa says, waving back over to him. "Don't be speeding off with my baby."

"I won't. I'm as safe as they come," he says as he smoothly backs out of the driveway.

"Uh huh. You better be." She says before entering her vehicle.

Further Down the street Arieus along with countless other kids walk to school. While most traveled in packs, Arieus is alone. In a perfect world Jalisa or Mike would drive him to school but of course this isn't a perfect world.

"Ay Black ass. You wanna ride?" screams Mike as he drives by.

Like always Arieus paid him no mind as he continues to his destination sluggishly walking, head to the ground. He looks up once he'd figured they were gone only to discover his mother riding by.

Avoiding him, she stares straight ahead. In her heart she knew it was no good reason why she couldn't drop him off at school. A small part of her even kind of wanted to. It's just that being alone with Arieus really wasn't something she was able to deal with just yet.

HONK HONK "Arieus the smelliest," shouts Mike, startling Arieus. He laughs hysterically after making his way back around the block once more just for the pure enjoyment of picking.

As the car turns the corner Arieus realizes that all of the kids who were walking in close vicinity of him had also turned the corner. There wasn't a soul in site. He was the last kid on the block.

Switching directions, he makes his way back over to the house. This time head to the sky, with a pep in his step. He scans the block as he walks, checking to see if any neighbors happened to be watching. The coast was clear.

After briskly walking, finally, he'd made it back to his home where he pulls out his key to unlock the door. Walking in, he drops his book bag onto the floor after pulling his best friend from inside.

Squeezing it tightly he creeps over to Tim's bedroom. The door is cracked, leaving lazy ass Tim visibly lying asleep, hand in his underwear, snoring like a freighttrain. Feeling bold Arieus pushes open the door, purposely loud enough to awaken him.

His tactic works. Tim quickly jumps up, wiping his eyes, squinting, making sure he wasn't dreaming. "Boy what the fuck you doing in my God damn room?" he says failing to notices the pistol in Arieus palms.

Arieus doesn't say a word. Instead he walks to the center of the mattress, staring directly at Tim.

"Motherfucker did you hear me? I said what the fuck you doing in here," Tim asked, maneuvering his body, now sitting up. "You got five seconds to get your little black ass outta here before I put one of these here crutches so far up your motherfucking ass."

Still silent, Arieus raises the pistol, pointing directly to Tim.

"Boy what the hell you doing?" Tim shouts, startled. "You better put that shit down. What the fuck is wrong with you?"

Arieus smiles.

"Boy what the fuck you doing? Now I know you got a lot going on and I haven't necessarily been the nicest guy in the world but I'm telling you right now. You're making a big mistake. Put the gun down," he pleads as he points his index finger to Arieus, demandingly.

Arieus smile fades as he lowers the gun.

"Yeah, that's right. I'm telling you if you do this, you'll regret it for the rest of your life. Not to mention you're going to prison. You think I'm bad wait till you go there. I've been, trust me. Just put the gun down."

Arieus stands still, gun pointed to the floor.

"Atta boy," Tim says. "Now just bring me the gun and I'll act like none of this ever happened. I promise--I promise," he says sincerely as Arieus stands in place. "Come on Son. Son. You know you're still my son. I just been showing you tough love," he says as he pounds his chest with his fist. "I don't mean nothing by it. I just don't want you to be some sort of coward. But I get it, I get it. I been too hard. Just bring me the gun son. Come on. Just bring me the gun."

Arieus steps closer to Tim as he reaches his right hand out.

"Yeah you're doing the right thing son. I'm sorry man. I'm sorry."

Arieus stops a few feet from Tim.

"Come on Son. Just give me the gun," Tim says, trying to regain the control he'd thought he'd had.

Arieus smiles again.

"What are you doing son? Just give me the gun."

Arieus cocks back, raising the gun once more.

"No. Son. No," Tim pleads as he throws his hands in the air attempting to block the bullets that were soon to be sent his way.

BOW BOW BOW

Arieus lets off three shots. Two to the chest, one to the head as his smile grows wider.

Tim lays in a pool full of blood, instantly dieing.

"Oh shit. Oh shit," screams Pete, hopping up and down excitedly. "That shit was Gangsta. I can't even lie. That shit was motherfucking gangsta. Cold blooded too," he says before looking over to Arieus, nodding his head in approval. "Fuck Tim," he shouts. "I knew it. I knew you was about to say that. That's crazy. Smoked that bitch ass cracker. Can't believe his ass tried to act like he was a changed man and shit. Who the fuck he think he was fooling. Trying to call you Son. Fuck outta here. How the fuck did you feel after you did that shit?"

"I felt reborn," responds Arieus as he continues staring up, speaking calmly. "I felt like a million pounds were lifted off of my shoulders. I had never felt better."

"No regrets? No remorse at all?" asks Pete.

"None."

"And nobody ever suspected you of doing it? I can't front I would have put two and together."

"Before I left I made sure I broke the back window to make it seem like that's where the murderer came in.

"Smart move."

"Tim wasn't just an asshole to us. He was an ass to everyone. Not to mention all of the guy's wife's he'd slept with over the years. Anybody could've found their way in that house and pulled that trigger."

"Damn. So how your fam act? I know how it was when my Pops died. Shit was rough."

"They cried as I suppose any other family in that situation would've did but I didn't give a damn. No one ever cared about my feelings. So all that crying was pointless. Fuck them."

"I'm saying though. Wasn't Tim paying most of the bills?"

"Yeah. I can't lie it did get pretty hard without Tim hustling around. My Mom worked fast food so she really aint have enough money to take care of all of us."

"Damn so how was that?"

"It really wasn't new to me. I was used to living like that. My sibling and Mother were the one's who had to adapt."

"So how did y'all survive?"

"My Mom met Ray. Everything kind of changed after that."

2002

Jalisa struts up to the door of the 'Park Place Community Rec Center' looking better than she had in years. Draped in a black skin tight dress, showing off the physique of a woman half her age, hair braided up neatly with accessories and heels perfectly matching to her dress. She's accompanied by Ray, a tall flamboyant Black man.

Now Ray wasn't exactly the nicest piece of eye candy. He had the face of Shabba Ranks and the body of Carl Winslow. Still, the way he talked, dressed and walked made up for it. Not only that, it's virtually impossible to forget to mention his jewelry. Ol school style. Three gold rings on each hand, gold bracelet on one wrist, Rolex on the other, while 4 gold chains sat around his neck that perfectly set off his never too dull gold tooth. Ray was a Mack from way back. Any woman down on her luck would look to him as an Angel.

Jalisa was no exception, she hadn't been treated well in so long that she didn't give a damn how attractive Ray was, he was everything she'd hoped for, everything she'd been dreaming of. Since the day he pulled over in his Pearl Mercedes CLK430 to assist her with a flat tire, in her mind she was his.

Initially Ray wasn't exactly the settling down type. After so many secret love affairs with married women he just couldn't see himself giving the opposite sex his all. Like most of the other women

Ray came across he saw Jalisa as just ass and titties, something he could fuck on for a little bit. Nothing major, after all, she was sexy. But after wining and dining her for a few weeks he quickly realized that she was just what he needed.

Jalisa was loyal, with a soothing spirit that led Ray to believe he could trust her. In time, she'd filled him in on the hell that Ray had put her through. This made him livid. No, not because of how he treated her but because Ray was a street nigga. He'd done a couple prison stints but a girl like Jalisa might have been what could have saved him. Not wasting a second, he fully invested in her. Whenever you saw Jalisa, you saw Ray. In just 6 months he was ready to do whatever it took not only to keep her around but to keep her happy. To him, just seeing the smile on her face was more valuable than gold. And after being informed that she'd never in her 36 years on earth had a birthday cake, let alone birthday party, Ray made it his duty to put a change to that.

"Where in the world is everybody? I can't believe we're so early," said Jalisa as the couple walk into the lobby of the rec center. To anyone else this may have appeared to be an obvious surprise party, but honestly Jalisa had no idea. When you're not use to being treated well, sometimes it's hard to imagine anyone going out of their way for you.

Besides, Ray had been telling her for weeks that his best friend was throwing a party, in her head she just assumed that they were early arrivals. Which of course she didn't have a problem with.

Hell, it was her birthday too, she was just happy to be actually getting out of the house. Usually birthdays were just another day. Over the years she'd even found herself taking Tim out to eat to celebrate, with him not even thinking to even so much as split the bill.

"Yeah I guess we are pretty early," replies Ray before opening up the double doors.

The room is pitch black for a quick second when out of the darkness, light appears! "Surprise," everyone shouted.

Classic. The look on Jalisa's face is priceless. "Oh my God," she screamed before leaping into Ray's flabby but sturdy arms. Tears fall from her face as she rejoices. Her eyes light as she gazes around at the professionally decorated gym, filled with colorful tables, balloons and even a banner that read 'Happy Birthday Jalisa!'

As the DJ cuts on the Stevie Wonder version of 'Happy Birthday' Ray looks into Jalisa's eyes "Happy Birthday Baby. I love you."

"Aww baby. I love you more. I can't believe this. All of this for me?" asked Jalisa, still in awe.

"Believe it baby. You deserve it," followed Ray before leaning in for a kiss.

Arieus along with Faith, Grace, Amanda, all 8 of Ray's young daughters, as well as all of the other many guests admire Jalisa and

Ray's love before everyone eventually made their way over to personally wish Jalisa a happy birthday.

Pushing through the crowd, Faith, Grace and Amanda make sure they are the first to greet their Mother. Of course Arieus stands in the cut unsure of why he was even in attendance. Well not really unsure, Ray had given him $50 to show up. The most money anyone had ever given him. Actually the most money he'd ever had. From his view he watched as his sisters finally met up with their Mother.

"Happy Birthday Mommy," says Amanda followed by Faith and Grace as they all hug, sharing a moment they would all cherish for the rest of their lives.

After everyone gets their hello's out of the way, Ray grabs Jalisa by the hand, escorting her to the dance floor. "Baby I don't know about you but I'm ready to party."

The crowd follows as Ray gets loose, putting his two left feet to work. He's off beat but it's not a bad thing. Actually it's pretty entertaining. His confidence was hypnotizing, resulting in nearly everyone in attendance standing to their feet, having the time of their life's.

Later in the evening after nearly exhausting himself and using his personality to host and ensure everyone was having a good time, Ray decides to hop on the microphone next to a table full of gifts.

"Yooo, Yooo." He says trying to get everyone's attention. It was a little tough, considering the fact, the party had been BYOB. "YOOOOO," he attempts again, this time gathering more attention but still not the entire crowd. He then motions for the DJ to cut the music. "Ay Motherfuckers I'm trying to say something," he screamed bringing things to a screeching halt. "That's more like it," he says before looking over to Jalisa, who was standing toward the back with a few of her new found friends. "Ay baby, come on up here," he says motioning with his hand for her to join him.

"Baby no," Jalisa says, whining in a childish tone as she blushed.

"Baby nothing. Come on. I got something to say."

"Baby," Jalisa says again not budging.

"Please baby," follows Ray, lip poked as the women in the crowd encourage her to join her man.

"Ok," Jalisa says finally giving in.

"Thank you baby," Ray replies pleasantly. "Look at my baby all fine and shit," he says into the microphone as Jalisa makes her way up, causing her face to brighten even more.

"You know I don't like all this attention," Jalisa says as she finally reaches Ray.

"Sorry baby. It's only going to take a second," he replies before grabbing her by the hand, staring deeply into her eyes. "Everybody in here knows I love Jalisa to death. Being with her has been the best 6 months of my life," he says into the microphone.

"Aww," says the crowd.

"The way she treats my girls with so much compassion. A person from the outside looking in wouldn't even have a clue that they weren't hers. It's beautiful. And I have to say, I love her kids too, Faith and Grace's beautiful smile. I love how Amanda is one of the most mature young women I've ever met. The way she takes care of little Cameron lets me know how great Jalisa raised her. And Arieus, well Arieus is just Arieus."

The crowd laughs as Ray's eyes remain focused on Jalisa.

"When I met you guys you were going through a really tough time and I admire how strong you were. I couldn't imagine my life without you and I'm not even sure how I ever lived without you on my side. With that being said," Ray says before dropping down on one knee, pulling out a small jewelry box as the crowd gasps. "Jalisa Anderson will you make me the luckiest man on earth and marry me?"

Instantly bursting into tears, Jalisa shouts, "Oh my God. Yes! Yes!"

Ray dresses her ring finger in a flawless 2 carat gold diamond ring as the guests cheer.

"I love you so much," says Ray before grabbing Jalisa, pulling her close.

"I love you more than anything," Jalisa follows, as the couple make love with their eyes.

"It's officially time to celebrate. Congratulations Ray and Jalisa," the DJ screams over the microphone as Jagged Edge's 'Let's Get Married Remix' turns up the party once again.

Thursday (cont...)

"Trays Gentleman. Trays," says Maine as he and Eric walk up.

"Bout God damn time," Pete says as he hops up, rubbing his belly. "Let me get that," he says as Maine slides a tray of bologna and cheese, with two slices of white bread and an orange to him. "Thanks bruh. I'm starving. We don't get a drink?" he asks.

"Naw they said they ran out of tea earlier," replies Eric.

"Damn, so y'all just gonna give me a dry ass bologna and cheese sandwich with nothing to wash it down? I cant keep drinking this nasty ass sink water. Who the fuck wants to keep drinking from the same place you piss at."

"Looks like you have no choice," follows Eric as Pete sits down on his bunk, shaking his head in disappointment.

"I assume you aint eating again today?" Maine asks Arieus as he slowly shakes his head.

"Yo let me get that," Pete says to Arieus.

"Why not," Arieus says never looking away from the ceiling.

"Hold the fuck up. Yall two in this bitch talking to one another? What the hell going on?" says Maine as he slides the other Tray through.

"Ay man. We just getting an understanding," follows Pete as he sits his tray down on his bed before getting up to retrieve his new one.

"Wow. I never would have saw that coming," says Maine.

"Hey. Me either," Pete says as he grabs a hold of the tray. "Sometimes you gotta get to know a person before you judge him. It's enough hate in this place. I don't have to add any to it," he says as he sits back down.

"You hear this motherfucker," Maine asks Eric.

"Yeah." Replies Eric.

"Matter fact, while I'm being all positive and shit," follows Pete, looking over to Eric. "I guess I gotta apologize to you about yesterday. I was acting off emotions. My bad," says Pete as he takes a large bite out of his sandwich.

"Yeah ok," says Eric, looking away.

"Yo whatsup with you?" asks Maine to Eric. "This guy just apologized to you and that's all you're gonna say?"

"I said ok. What you want me to do? Suck his dick?"

"It's cool," replies Pete, speaking with a mouth full. "I know I did my part, my conscience is good, that's all that matters."

"Alright, well holla if you need us," says Maine.

"Bet," replies Pete as Maine and Eric walk away, talking among themselves. "Yo now get back to that Motherfucking story. Did they ass ever get married?" Pete asks before taking another large bite from his sandwich.

"Yep. Nice wedding. Ray even got my Mom's family to come through."

"Damn shit was really looking up."

"Yeah they were," replies Arieus.

Christmas was never really anything too special for the Andersons. Yeah, they put up a puny little tree and even had a few cheap last minute gifts thrown underneath but for the most part it was just a regular day. No Egg nog, Christmas Carols or anything else of the sort was ever thrown into the mix.

Of course 'Super' Ray made it his responsibility to swoop down and change the game. Growing up in the projects, Christmas was always the best time of the year for him, they were dirt poor so any gift they received was greatly appreciated. Still, it really wasn't the gifts that made this time of the year so grand. It was the love, family from all over would come down; Cousins, Aunties and everyone would pile up at Grandma's house to enjoy their time together.

To Ray nothing was more important than family, not the money, not the cars, nothing. Reason being, he'd lived without all of those things before but had yet to live without family.

Sadly, after the death of his Grandma, things had sort of changed. All of his cousins had families of their own with new Christmas time agenda's. The love was still there but gone were the days of them all meeting up on Christmas Eve.

Wanting desparately to continue the tradition, he and his older brother Carl decided they'd simply celebrate on their own. With their Mom dying and no other siblings they figured this was the best way to keep their immediate family intact.

Although Carl only had 1 kid, Ray had 8, so it still kind of gave the brothers that old school feeling of when they were kids with a packed house full of cousins. In fact, the new arrangement may have even been better than before. Grandma had a two bedroom shack, yeah they had a blast but it was always a struggle finding a comfortable spot to sleep at night.

Those problems were long gone. Carl owned an immaculate 6 bedroom crib in Virginia Beach, equipped with a pool, back yard basketball court, and even an inside gym. Carl was living large.

As they stepped into the home you'd think Jalisa and her kids were inside of the white house. Their jaws dropped to the freshly polished hardwood floor as they stared in awe of their temporary residence. This was totally different from anything they'd seen. They were the same family who'd never even so much as traveled two hours out of the city. Hell, the only time they ever even stayed in hotels were the times they'd been evicted from one of their many cribs. And of course those were always the bed bug infested, $25 a night type.

"Welcome to the Crib," said Carl as Ray's extra-large family stepped into his domain. The voices from Rays 8 young children overshadow Jalisa's kids, as they stood, feet planted admiring all of the beautiful paintings and sculptures perfectly placed along the house. "Ah man bro I didn't know you were going to bring this many people. I don't think I have enough room for everyone. Somebody's gotta go," says Carl jokingly.

"Come on bro I told you I had a few extra guests, don't do us like that," Ray replied.

"Ok. I could never throw any women or children on the street. And you're my brother so I guess I can't throw you to the streets either. No matter how bad I want to. But you," he says pointing over to Arieus. "You might have to go. You look like a damn grown man. Bigger than me."

Embarrassed, Arieus's head drops to the floor, attempting to duck the attention. But at 6'3 and so dark that he was nearly blue it was virtually impossible not to stand out. "Naw I'm just kidding," adds Carl, noticing that he'd made Arieus uncomfortable. "Ray aint tell you about my sense of humor? I get crazy sometimes. Especially when I'm drunk. And I gotta confession to make. I'm drunk," he says laughing. "But hey it's the holidays what do you expect," says Carl walking up to Ray and his family.

"It's cool Carl. I already told everybody not to expect a damn thing from you. They already know you aint shit," Rays says as he and his brother embrace.

110

Everyone laughs. "Well at least they know, I'd hate to have to surprise them. But naw seriously I got all the beds made up and rooms ready," he says as he gives out hugs to his many guests. "It's plenty of room for y'all. Well at least for the girls," he says before pausing in front of Arieus. "Arieus you don't mind bunking with my boy do you?" he asks, pointing to his 7 year old son Kanan, who was sitting at the top of the stairs having an intense conversation with a pair of his action figures. "Since you and your little brother are the only other boys I didn't think it would be a problem."

"It's cool," says Arieus never looking up.

"Remember we got cameras in the room. Don't try nothing with my boy. I don't trust shit," he follows still not moving away from Arieus.

"Carl shut the fuck up aint nobody gon touch your boy," blurts Ray as his 8 girls run up to their rooms, dragging Faith, Grace and Amanda along.

"Nigga I'm just being safe," he says looking over to Ray. "No offense. I'm really just joking. But in a serous way. A way so serious that if I even suspect anything crazy going on, somebody's gonna die," he says focusing on Arieus.

Soon everyone gets squared away into their rooms as Christmas music blasts through the house.

Needless to say Arieus decides not to mingle. In fact he hated the place already. It wasn't so much of the things that Carl had said that had made him upset, he was Teflon to words. Like always, it was the unwanted attention. He didn't want to be anywhere near Carl in fear that more would be cast upon him. His blood boiled each time he heard the sound of Carl's loud obnoxious laugh echo through the house.

The fact that he was stuck in the room with his four year old brother and Kanan didn't make anything better. Back home he shared a room with Cameron but he'd learned to drown him out. Ignoring two kids was hard though. Especially with Kanan's annoying obsession with Santa Clause, he couldn't go ten seconds without mentioning the guy.

"Hey Arieus, I can't wait for Santa. Hey Arieus, what's Santa going to get you? Hey Arieus, do you think Santa wears long johns under his red suit? I know he has to be pretty cold up there." The questions were never ending. Even as Arieus attempted to answer as vaguely as possible or sometimes not at all, Kanan still kept going and going.

It took everything he had inside of him not to look at the kid and say, "Motherfucker it aint no damn Santa. Don't your little dumbass see all them God Damn presents under the tree. Who the fuck you think bought them?"

112

Lucky for Kanan Arieus had some type of heart, he still remembered being a kid believing in Santa himself. But after being disappointed by him and his other Fairy Tale friends year after year, he soon grew a sort of hatred for them. He didn't feel the need to make Kanan feel his animosity so he instead played along, no matter how annoying it was growing to be.

"Everybody come eat, Brunch is served," shouts Carl from downstairs.

"Thank God, I'm starving," says Kanan as he rushes to the door.

"Me too, I'm starving," follows Cameron. He was now at the age where he repeated everything other people said.

As they exited the room Arieus continued staring up at the ceiling, off in his own world. Although his stomach was touching his back, being close to Carl just wasn't worth it.

"Yo Arieus. You aint eating?" asks Ray as he barged into the room

"No. I'm good," Arieus replies never looking up.

"You sure? We got everything you need or want, pancakes, sausage, french toast. Got it all catered from 'The Breakfast Bistro.' Everybody knows that they food is the motherfucking truth," says Ray still standing at the door.

"No I'm alright."

"Ok," Ray follows as he shuts the door halfway before quickly pushing it back open. "Ay Arieus, you mind if we talk for a second?"

Arieus looks over to Ray confused. This wasn't a typical question that he'd been asked. Usually no one ever wanted to talk to him and if they did, they just did it, they didn't ask. "Uh yeah," Arieus agrees, as he sits up on the bed placing his feet to the floor.

Shutting the door, Ray strolls in, plopping down on Kanans bed across from Arieus. "Look man. I know you damn near a grown ass man. So I aint coming in here trying to be your Daddy. But I do want you to know I'm here. I aint have no Pops growing up. My Mom married a lame ass nigga who aint say two words to me. I hated that shit. So I refuse to be one of them dudes. I just want you to know I'm here. You ever got any problems, come to me for anything. Big or small," he says as he and Arieus make eye contact for a brief second. "Once I married your Mom I took on responsibility for yall. And I always take care of my responsibilities. I got your back. You aint gonna never have to worry about me even thinking about doing any of the bullshit that bitch ass motherfucker Tim did. Trust me," he says looking at Arieus, waiting for him to look up once again. Once he did, Ray extended his arm for a fist bump. This was another thing Arieus had never done. Shocked, he slowly balled up his fist before tapping Ray's. "Well I'ma go get something to eat. He says before standing to his feet. "You know you're welcome to as much as you'd like. Don't mind my brother, he's been a hater all his life. He don't mean no harm though," Ray says before walking out of the door, shutting it behind him.

The remainder of the day things are pretty good. Everyone's having a ball; drinking, smoking and eating. After a while, Arieus even decides to come down stairs, his hunger pains had grown unbearable.

"Look who decided to come down," says Carl. "I thought you was a mute or something. Aint said a word ever since you got here."

Annoyed and fed up, Arieus still manages to crack a smile. He didn't want the attention but he'd realized that Carl was like a Dog, he attacked harder whenever he could sense fear.

"And the motherfucker still aint said a word," Carl says looking over to Jalisa. "What you drop this one on his head or something when he was born?" he asks as Jalisa and Amanda both laugh as they sit relaxing on Carl's leather couch watching his Big Screen T.V.

"Ay nigga, leave my son alone. He aint bothering nobody," says Ray, buttings in. He too is sitting on the couch.

"Yes the fuck he is. It's always them quiet black ass motherfuckers who the sneakiest," Carl barks before looking over to Arieus. "What you been thinking about upstairs all day? Blowing up the place?"

Jalisa and Amanda laugh once again.

"Nigga I said leave him alone," bolts in Ray as Arieus slowly walks to the kitchen.

"Ray shut your ass up. That boy damn near grown, if he want me to shut up he knows how to talk," Carl fires back.

"Motherfucker it aint got nothing to do with him no more. I said shut up," Ray says as he emphasizes the word 'I'. "How about that."

"Or what?" Carl barks back.

"Or I'ma beat your ass just like that faggot did back in the day,"

"See nigga why you gotta go there?" Carl asks, almost instantly changing his mood, nearly dropping his cup of Remi and coke.

"Cause nigga, I told your ass to shut up. You don't never listen."

The two siblings went back in forth for a while like brothers do but not one more word was spoken about Arieus. Ray had successfully kept his word. He had Arieus's back. This was the first time in life anyone had ever defended and acted as if they cared about him.

Arieus didn't stay down stairs for long, he made a plate, ate at the kitchen table and left. But what he did do was grow an appreciation for Ray. No, he didn't trust him with his life or anything. Someone who'd been tortured as much as he'd been could never fully trust anyone. Especially that quick. Still, he did feel a lot better about the guy.

"Hey Arieus. Do you hear that?" asks Kanan as he stood on the side of Arieus's bed. It was the middle of the night and everyone had long gone to sleep.

"Huh? Hear what?" asked Arieus still half asleep.

"I hear someone outside. I think it may be Santa," says Kanan, excitedly.

"I don't hear anybody," Arieus answers before turning away from Kanan.

"I'm serious Arieus," Kanan says as he nudges Arieus's shoulder. "Can you please come downstairs and check with me? Please. I'm begging you I've been waiting for this moment all of my life."

"No," follows Arieus, still not budging.

"Please Arieus," he says nudging at his shoulder a little harder. "I don't want to meet him by myself. I'll have no proof that I really saw him. I need ya Arieus."

117

"No," Arieus responds once again. This time with extra base in his voice.

"Ok. Cool. If that's how you want it. That's how you're going to get it," says Kanan. "Come on. We're going on an Adventure to meet Santa," he says looking over to Cameron. He'd woken him up before he'd talked to Arieus.

"Yayy," says Cameron, throwing his hands to the air as he hopped out of bed.

"Shhh," whispers Kanan with his index finger over his mouth "We can't wake anyone up. This is a top notch mission. Kids all over the world have been trying for centuries to do what we're about to do. This is big. We can't mess this up."

"Gotcha," says Cameron after placing his index finger over his mouth.

Kanan then runs over to his toy box before handing Cameron a pair of Ninja Turtle Sunglasses. "Here take these. There my new night vision goggles. This will help us navigate our way through downstairs. It might get tricky in the dark," say Kanan "You ready?"

"Yeah," whispers Cameron as he throws his pretend Night Vision goggles on upside down.

"Good lets do this," he says before giving Cameron a high five. "Wish me luck. I might need it," he says looking over to Arieus who'd already fallen fast asleep.

118

Cameron follows Kanans lead as they creep out of the room, headed down stairs on their way to successfully complete the top notch mission.

"Aha!" says Kanan as they finally make it to the first floor. He looks over to the cookies in milk he'd left Santa. "The snacks are still intact. He has to still be outside. There's no way Santa would be able to resist."

Cameron nods his head.

"Hold on, let me make sure there not stale, I don't wanna make Santa upset," says Kanan before walking over to the table to take a bite. "Oh there good. Real good," he says chomping away, dropping crumbs onto the floor.

"I want a piece," says Cameron, forgetting to speak quietly.

"SHHH," whispers Kanan, once again throwing his index finger to his lips. "No, this was for experimental purposes only. This isn't a game. This is serious business. Fix your glasses," he says as Cameron nods his heads and turns his glasses right side up. "I got an idea. Come with me." They creep over to the chimney. "We might be able to catch him right in the act," says Kanan as they continue making their way over to the chimney before Cameron trips over a shoe, falling to the floor making unnecessary noise. "SHHH," whispers, Kanan once again as he helps Cameron up. "What's wrong with you, why aren't you using your night vision goggles the way that you're supposed to?"

"I don't know," answers Cameron, nonchalantly.

"You can't ruin this for us," he says as they finally make it over to the fireplace where Kanan drops to his knees to takes a peek up. He stares for a second before realizing that he doesn't see anything. "Nope nothing up there," he says before standing back to his feet. "Only one other choice now. Obviously he's still on the roof," he says before pausing, looking around suspiciously. "SHHH," he says again. "I can hear them. We gotta go outside. You scared Cameron?"

Cameron shakes his head with a smile.

"Good," you're gonna cherish this memory for the rest of your life. We might even get famous. No kid has ever done what we're about to do. Come on," he whispers as they tip toe over to the front door, twisting the knob lightly. After making sure he made as little noise as possible, he quietly opens up.

"Freeze get on the ground," screams an FBI agent, pointing a gun to the head of Cameron and Kanan, causing both kids to scream, throwing both hands to the ceiling as dozens of squad cars and Detectives surround the house.

"Hold up one motherfucking minute," says Pete as he sits down on his bed, feet to the floor. "What the fuck just happened?" he asks before standing up to look at Arieus as they talk.

"Yeah, I think I may have left out a key fact. Ray and his brother were two of the biggest cocaine distributors in all of Virginia," speaks Arieus, head to the ceiling.

"What? Foreal? Your mama fucked around and married the plug?"

"I guess that's what you call it. How do you think Carl got the big ass crib? Ray might've had a crib like that too but the guy had so many kids I guess he just didn't care about shit like that."

"Damn. Hearing you say that just made me think about somebody."

"Who?"

"DaDa. He was just like Ray and his brother. Big time drug dealer. He was involved in my case."

"So I'm guessing he's in prison too?"

"Nope. The moment the Feds snatched me up his ass fled the country. Aint nobody seen or heard from him since. I think about him

121

all the time though. Wherever he at, it gotta be better than how I'm living," says Pete. "But yeah, back to your story. That's crazy that they arrested Ray just when you was starting to like the nigga."

"Yep. That alone sorta taught me that good things that come in life are only temporary. I hadn't quite lost all hope for humanity but as far as anyone in Virginia was concerned I was convinced that they were the Devil."

"Damn so how did your Mom take it? Just when she was finally happy."

"I really don't know. She went to jail too"

"What?" Pete shouts. "Aw shit that's even crazier. This shit getting better and better. I need some motherfucking popcorn."

"Yeah they say she was a mule. Went to the feds for four years, while Ray and his brother got life."

"So where the hell y'all go at? Wont you only 16?"

"I was 17. Almost 18 but almost didn't count. So I was sent off to Foster care."

"Damn all of y'all went?"

"Well Amanda was already of age so she she stayed with friends. Faith and Grace moved in with Tim's family along with Cameron."

"So you aint never get to see them again?"

"Nope not for years."

"Ok let me ask you this," says Pete still staring over to Arieus. "Did it ever cross your mind that this was kind of your fault? After all you are the one who killed Tim."

"I guess you could say that but if you're asking if I ever sat around crying about the shit. Hell no," he says finally looking over to Pete before returning his attention back to the ceiling.

"So you basically saying they deserved it?"

"Pretty much."

"Alright so judging from what's been going on so far in your life. Is it safe to say Foster Care was just as bad as everything else?"

"Yeah. It's safe to say that. But I keep telling you I'd grown immune. Maybe it would have been harder for a regular 17 year old but to me it was just another day in the life."

"So what about school? Wasn't you in the 12th grade by then?"

"Yep."

"Still doing good?

"Of course."

"So going to college to be a teacher was still the plan I see," Pete says as he flops back onto his bed.

"Well actually, I'd outgrown the the thought of being a teacher but I could never stop thinking going away to college. I had a goal to accomplish and it was so close by then, I could taste it."

Suburban State University, in the small city of Ramona, Kansas, thousands and thousands of miles away from Virginia. Perfect. Just how Arieus always wanted things to be.

It was the first day of school and the air was warm and inviting. New students, returning students, parents and sibling all walked through the brilliantly landscaped schoolyard laughing, joking and enjoying their last moments together. Looking at the many faces scattered around it was impossible to find an unpleasant one.

That was until Arieus pulled up. He along with his signature emotionless stare stepped out of his taxi, alone, no parents, grandparents nor siblings, all he had was himself. Not that he cared, he'd grown to be strong, ready for anything that would come his way. The time was finally here. The time he could re-invent himself. He'd never had a chance to start over, and here it was. Taking a whiff of the air he was set to breathe for the next several years, he paid his driver with his earnings from his summer job as a dishwasher at Golden Coral back home, grabbed his two bags from out the trunk, and made his way to the GEORGE WASHINGTON building. He'd been assigned to dwell there for the duration of his freshman year.

Butterflies consumed his body as the thought sunk in that his dream had actually became a reality. With a life full of hardships he was now fully prepared to forget the past and move on to a life filled with limitless happiness. August 16, 2003 was now his birthday, the day his life would official began.

Meanwhile in the dorm, Arieus's new roommate, Tyler Cooper, a boyishly handsome 18 year old white kid stood with his middle aged parents, Kate and Tom.

"I think it's time to go honey," said Tom looking over to his wife.

"I'm not ready yet," she whined.

"Mom calm down I'm only 30 minutes away from home," says Tyler.

"I know but I'm gonna miss you so much," she said before hugging Tyler, tightly. "I'm gonna miss you," she repeats.

"I'm gonna miss you too Mama," says Tyler as he looks over to his Dad, they both roll their eyes.

"Are you sure you bought everything you need?" asks Kate as she backs away from Tyler, now holding his right hand staring sweetly into his eyes?

"Honey I'm sure he's ok," butts in Tom. "Anything he forgot he can come home anytime he wants and get it."

"Oh my God. I'm just gonna miss you so much," she says.

"Come on honey," Tom says as he tugs his wife along.

"Ok mom I'm gonna miss you too. I'll walk you guys to your car," says Tyler as all three walk towards the door.

"Make sure you call me every day," she says as she stares at her baby boy.

"Ok Mom."

"And make sure you brush your teeth and wash your face before you go to sleep at night," she says as they enter the hallway.

"Mom, I know, I know," says Tyler.

Literally seconds after their departure, Arieus arrives. A huge grin appears, showing his perfectly aligned pearly white teeth. He never exposed them much but the way he was feeling, he was quite sure he'd be putting them to use a lot more often.

Dropping his bags to the floor, he paused, gazing around his new room, taking it all in.

Noticing Tyler's bags, he hopes that he's nothing like his last roommate from the Foster home, 'Mike Laterno.' To put it simple, Mike was a pervert, he was a little white 16 year old accused child molester whose penis grew rock hard at the worst times. It wasn't anything for Arieus to walk into the kitchen and see Mike naked from the ass down, dick in hand whacking away in the middle of the afternoon. Even as Arieus made his presence known, Mike would only turn around, looking as if Arieus was in the wrong. Soon Arieus just stopped coming out of his room unless it was to go to school.

However as Arieus picked up a picture of Tyler chilling with some friends from off of the dresser, it was clear he probably wasn't the Mike Laterno type. Actually he looked like the type who'd never have to masturbate a day in his life. It was only a picture but just from that alone it was clear as day to see that this guy was a chick magnet. It was written all over his face.

"Roomie," Tyler shouts as he enters back into the room, discovering Arieus still holding his picture up.

Arieus drops the picture. "Oh hey," he says startled.

"What's up Man? What's your name?" asks Tyler as he gleefully walks over.

"Arieus."

"Arieus?" he says before giving him a high five. "Man that's the coolest fucking name I've ever heard. How the fuck I get stuck with Tyler," he follows as he shakes his head. "Where you from Man?"

"Virginia."

"Fucking Virginia. I heard they got some killer waves down in Virginia Beach. That's fucking cool ass shit," he says as he nods his head. "I'm from here. Born and raised. I should've went out of state for college. But I couldn't get into anywhere else. My Dad knows the Dean around here, so you already know how that goes."

"Yeah," says Arieus, lying. Honestly he had know idea 'how it goes'. Not a clue. He for damn sure didn't have one single family member who could get him into anywhere besides jail.

"You here alone? Your parents didn't come?" asks Tyler, looking around.

"Yeah I'm by myself," says Arieus, embarrassed.

"Dude," Tyler screams. "Man that's fucking cool as hell. I wish I could've came alone. My parents are fucking humiliating," he says. "Man this is about to be the best times we're ever gonna have. I heard it's a party tonight. You tryna roll?"

"No. I think I'm gonna stay here."

"Stay here? Are you fucking crazy? Have you seen all the hot chicks galloping around?" he asks as he holds both of his hands towards his chest, in a juggling motion as if they were a woman's breast.

"Not tonight maybe another time," Arieus follows.

"Sorry man but I just can't take no for an answer. As your roommate it's my obligation to make sure you live this fucking college life to the fullest."

"N--" Arieus start to speak.

129

"Sorry man you're going," Tyler says, flashing a smile.

Nelly's Hot in Here blasts from an old two story frat house. This would make for the perfect scene for one of those 90's teen movies.

Arieus and Tyler both walk up to the front door as a few other young adults stand around the yard, drinking, chilling and talking amongst themselves.

"You alright man?" asks Tyler.

Arieus nods, as he peeps his surroundings. This was brand new to him. His heart thumped as he thought of the best ways to fit in. Nothing came to mind.

"I know everybody in here man. I've been coming to these parties since I was in the 11th grade. We're about to get so fuckin hammered. You know how to play beer pong right/" asks Tyler, over the loud music.

"Beer Pong?" asks Arius.

"Man I gotta teach you how to live."

They stroll inside the party. Arieus's heart pumps harder than before. So hard that he looks down to his chest to see if it was possible that anyone else could see it. Never in his life had he witnessed anything of the sort. White bitches everywhere. Dancing, drinking, mingling, singing, just having the time of their lives. He swallows a batch of spit as his body stiffens. In his head he told himself 'This is what you wanted Arieus. Be calm.' It was easier said than done.

"Oh my God! This party is fucking Amazing," says Tyler as he off beat bops along to the music.

Beau and Kevin, two young white preppy college students approach them clutching two beer cans a piece.

"Dude," Beau screams.

"Whatsup," says Tyler as the two embrace. "You motherfuckers ready to party," Tyler shouts over the loud music before pulling a zip lock bag full of marijuana from his pocket.

"Hell yeah," say Beau and Kevin in Unison.

"I got the papers. Let's go outside," says Kevin as they walk towards the door.

"Hold on guys," says Tyler, stopping. "I forgot to introduce you motherfuckers to my roommate," he says before pointing over to Arieus. "Arieus this is Kevin and Beau. Coolest fucking guys you're ever going to meet. We been boys since elementary. These guys are some fucking party animals. You're gonna fucking love them."

"Whatsup Dude," says Beau, excitedly.

"What's up Brother," follows Kevin in his token black guy voice.

"What's up," says Arieus as the three embrace.

"Well now that everyones acquainted lets go get high, Motherfuckers," Tyler joyfully shouts.

They walk around to the back yard where they spot four vacant lawn chairs. "Perfect," says Beau as they stroll over and choose their seats.

"Yo do you see the fucking babes in that motherfucker?" says Tyler as he passes the bag of weed over to Beau to roll.

"Nigga do we," Replies Beau.

"Dude," says Tyler, shocked.

"What?" asks Beau as Tyler nods over to Arieus. "Oh shit my bad dog. I don't mean anything by it. I'm so fucking sorry," he pleads to Arieus.

"It's cool," says Arieus, unbothered.

"You sure?" asks Beau.

"Yeah. It's cool," answers Arieus.

"So are you saying, we can just say it anytime we want or something?" asks Kevin.

132

"Yeah. I guess. I don't care," replies Arieus.

"See man I knew I was gonna like you," Beau says as he and Arieus high five. "Most black guys would want to kick my fucking ass."

"Hell yeah," says Tyler.

"Yeah. I just don't get it. If you guys say it's used as a term or endearment now, why can't we say it?" questions Beau.

"Yeah. It's not like we add the 'Er; to the end or anything," follows Kevin.

"Yeah, that would be crossing line," follows Tyler.

"Hell yeah. I'd never cross the line," says Beau.

"Fuck no," adds Kevin.

"Yeah we're totally respectful. It's just that, these are my niggas," adds Beau, pointing over to Tyler and Kevin. "My homies, my road dogs. Why can't every black guy think like you?"

At once they all look over to Arieus as if he somehow had an enlightening speech to lay on them or something. Realizing they were in search of feedback Arieus thinks quickly. "Yeah, it's just a word. I wasn't even born when people were getting called that."

"Exactly," follows Tyler.

"Neither were we. I can't help what my ancestors did hundreds of years ago." says Kevin.

In his head Arieus remembers the times not only Tim but Tim's entire family calling him nigger. But this was hardly the time nor place to speak on the subject. Not that he would have anyway. Instead, he chose to focus on the fact that the guys actually seemed to like him. Even if they would've added the 'er' it still wouldn't have mattered to him. He'd been through far too much to let that ruin his new life. Fuck that.

"Dude are you done with that joint or what?" asks Tyler, to Kevin.

"Yep," says Kevin as he lights it before placing it up to his lips. "Oh man this is some good shit right here," he follows after taking a drag.

"Come on dog you know I only fuck with the best. I got it from my nigga Tommy. He always has some fire on deck."

"Oh yeah. I forgot about Tommy," says Beau as Kevin passes the joint to Arieus.

Not wanting to seem like too much of a lame, Arieus puffs but never inhales, he even musters up a false cough to give off the illusion that he was down.

Over the course of the next hour the three teens had smoked a few more joints and had talked about everything from sports to how they were going to somehow take over the school. Before long it was time to head back inside to get white boy wasted.

No more than fifteen minutes after reentering the party a huge crowd surrounded Tyler and Eric, a chubby white sophomore.

"CHUG, CHUG, CHUG," the crowd chants.

Tyler and Eric stand next to one another as nozzles connected to beer kegs hang out of their mouths. With each passing second Eric appears as if he was on the virge of passing out as splashes of beer spills out the side of his mouth onto the collar of his plaid button up shirt. At the same time Tyler gulps confidently showing no signs of letting up until finally after giving it all he had, unable to compete, Eric throws in the towel.

"Yeah," Tyler screams as he raises his hands in triumph. "I'm the greatest," he shouts over the music as tens of other students run over to him.

Arieus stands off to the side holding a beer he'd only sipped once. It was the first sip he'd ever taken and for the life of him he couldn't figure out why the fuck people actually drunk them. It was disgusting. He didn't care how much so called fun getting wasted was, if he had to taste something as awful as that, you could count him out. Still, he knew people would wonder why he was in a party such as the one he was in, not drinking, so he figured he'd just hold on to it all night. For all they knew it could have been his 10th one, 99% of everyone in attendance was too drunk to tell anyway.

"Dude, I'm fucking wasted," says Tyler to Arieus, after escaping the crowd and walking over to him.

"Yeah, me too," Arieus lies.

"So why the fuck you sitting over here in the corner like a fucking loser? Do I have to mention again how many hot babes there are in here?" Tyler says as he drunkenly points out onto the crowd. "Do you fucking see, what I see?" he slurs. "Hottie heaven."

"I mean--" Arieus says.

"Hold that thought," says Tyler. "You see that group of bitches over there?" asks Tyler as he looks to the far left of the room.

"Yeah," says Arieus as he looks over.

"That's Stacey, Lisa, Becka, and Jill. I know Jill. I've been trying to bang her for years. And guess what to night is."

"What?" asks Arieus.

"My lucky fucking night. That's what the fuck it is. See, while you were over here keeping your ball sack warm, I was over there setting up plays for later on. Becka and Lisa both got their own crib. Yep own spot. And they invited me and a few friends of my choice over to Lisa's for a little late night 'chill' session," Tyler says, winking his eye at Arieus. "You know what that means right."

"Uh," says Arieus, hesitantly. "You're going to chill with them?"

"Fuck no. I aint doing no damn chilling. Anytime I go over to a chick's crib with no parents for miles away, after twelve. It's only one thing on my mind. Boning," he says pointing down to his crotch. "Yep, it's time to get it on. And guess who I've decided to bring with me?" he asks as he pats Arieus on the back.

"Who?" questions Arieus.

He wasn't stupid. He knew exactly who Tyler was talking about. Who else could it be? Only problem was, he was scared shitless. For obvious reasons. He thought of ways to get around it. But like always nothing came to mind.

"You fool," Tyler answered. "Well actually you, Beau and Kevin. Boy this shit is about to be fucking epic. Who knows they might get so fucking trashed that we end up having a friggin orgy or something," he say excitedly. "And just to think, we got plenty more nights just like this ahead of us," he says as throws his arm around Arieus's shoulder. "This right here," he says pointing back and forth between he and Arieus. "This right here, is the start of something great. You with me?"

"Yeah I'm with you," Arieus says, trying, but failing to join in on the excitement.

"Hell yeah," Tyler screams. "I'm about to go find dumb ass 1 and 2 and let them know the plan. "Woooooo," he screams once more as he walks away.

Standing alone, Arieus ponders just how the hell he had gotten himself in so deep. Yeah he wanted a new life but he never knew it would all happen so quickly. He wasn't ready. Zoning out, still thinking of how he could somehow get the hell out of the predicament, he mistakenly drops his beer to the ground causing it to splash in several directions, including the shoes of some brolic white guy, Matt, who just so happened to be walking out of the party with his girlfriend.

"Yo what the fuck," Matt shouts.

"I'm sorry," says Arieus, apologetic.

"You damn right you're sorry. Now wipe my God damn shoe off," the guy says stepping closer into Arieus's personal space.

"Huh?" asks Arieus, frantically thinking of his next move.

"You heard me. Wipe my God damn shoe off," Matt repeats.

Arieus stands still. This was a tough one. He knew he couldn't step into college letting people think they could run all over him. This could ruin everything he had planned. But he also didn't want people thinking he was just some thug ass black guy.

Fortunately, he didn't have to think too long as Tyler, Beau and Kevin came to his rescue.

"Hey Man what's the fucking problem?" asks Tyler, aggressively.

"What? What do you mean what's the problem?" Matt says turning around to Tyler, still angry as his girl watched from the side? "Your little fucking friend spilled beer all over my damn shoe."

"And," followed Kevin.

"And he needs to clean it off of me," Matt says, switching his attention over to Kevin.

"Dude. Who the fuck do you think you are?" follows Tyler, as he stepped to the side of the guy.

"Yeah," said Beau, following in his friends lead, stepping to the other side, while Arieus stood behind.

Looking around, Matt quickly realized he was surrounded.

"Yeah. You didn't know he had homies out here that have his back," says Tyler as Matt stands, still portraying himself as a tough guy. "I suggest you just move on along before shit gets out of hand. I'd hate for that to happen," says Tyler.

"Fuck," Matt screams after looking around once more. "Come on baby," he says after squeezing through the fellas and grabbing his girl by the hand, storming out of the party.

"Yeah motherfucker," says Kevin.

"Yeah, we showed that nigga," followed Beau as he and Kevin high five.

"Yep, you mess with one, you mess with us all. See, Arieus, we got your back," says Tyler before giving him a high five..

Not even 24 hours into college and Arieus had already met friends who cared about him. Just a second ago he was upset about how quickly things were moving but now it all seemed to be worth it. Well almost, this was before he realized the time to meet up with the girls was closer than he'd thought.

"Now that we got that loser out of the way. Let's get ready to have some real fun," says Tyler as he looks in the direction of the four girls. Their all staring over to the guys, non-discreet, flirting with their eyes.

One girl, Becka, actually stared at Arieus in a way he'd never been looked at before. She was beautiful. Bright red hair, with a body of a Goddess. Her looks made Arieus uneasy. No girl of her caliber had ever taken notice to him in such a way. No girl at all to be truthful.

It wasn't like Arieus was some ugly dude or anything. Actually he was far from it. Most would even call him handsome. Over the years he'd grown into his features and his acne had become nonexistent. Problem was, back home, no girl wanted to bone 'Arieus the Smelliest', no matter how good he looked. Plus you can't forget to mention the fact that he was quite possibly the worse dresser in the world growing up. Still was, it's just that white people really don't put as much enfaces on dressing like blacks do, so right about now he fit right in.

Still, unknowing of how to react, Arieus cowardly dropped his head.

"Yo their staring right at us," says Kevin as he Tyler and Beau gaze back at the beautiful women.

"Yeah what we waiting for? Let's go get them," says Beau.

"Say no more fellas, say no more," adds Tyler as he motions for the gang to follow him over to the girls.

"First day of college and already about to get laid. I always dreamed it would be like this," says Beau.

After making it back to Lisa's crib things were going great, there was alcohol, bud, and laughter. Everyone paired up and things seemed to be going just how they were supposed to. The mood was just right.

That was only until you took a look over to Arieus and Becka. Since arriving they were the only couple who'd failed to say more than a sentence to one another, nor had Arieus laid a single finger on her.

Tyler and Jill, Stacey and Beau, Kevin and Lisa; all sat spreaded across the living room making out as Arieus and Becka sat silently twiddling their thumbs. Time dragged and soon Becka could no longer stand the awkwardness. It was only so much she could take. She too was a freshman and had waited all of her life to fuck a black guy and this is the treatment she gets? Fuck that, fed up with Arieus and his childish ways, she stood to her feet, she was outta there. "I think I'm gonna go home. I'm tired," said Becka, straining out an obviously fake yawn as everyone looked over to her.

"Come on, we just got here," says Tyler, eyes low.

"Nah, I'm really tired," follows Becka. "I've been up since about five this morning."

"So. We all have," replies Beau.

"Sorry, I just gotta go," she says as she begins to walk to the door.

"Need me to walk you home?" asks Stacey.

"No, I'm Ok. It's not far at all."

"What? Becka are you crazy. It's 3:00 in the morning," follows Lisa, after taking a look at her wrist watch.

"Guys it's cool I only stay about two courts down. Trust me nothing will happen to me. I have pepper spray and a taser in my purse if anything does. I'm a big girl."

"Pepper spray and a Taser? What the hell is that gonna do to some sex crazed maniac," asks Stacey as the guys all looked over to one another angrily.

"Yeah, Becka we're going to walk with you," says Jill, readjusting herself to stand.

"Wait, wait, hold on, hold on," says Tyler, grabbing Jill before she could get to her feet. "Why can't ol Arieus walk you home?"

"Yeah, why cant he walk her?" Kevin asks before looking over to Arieus, only for him to instantly turn his head.

"It's ok," Becka says after noticing Arieus's reaction. "It's not that far. I can go alone. It's really not a problem. Thanks for caring guys but I told you, I'm a big girl. I'm good."

"No Becka someone has to walk with you," Lisa says hesitantly, looking over to Kevin.

"Yeah, like Tyler said though. What's wrong with my man Arieus? He's a perfect gentleman," says Kevin.

"Yeah," followed Beau with the co-sign. "You'll walk her right?" he asks bringing all attention over to Arieus once again.

"Uh--yeah-- yeah I'll do it." Arieus stutters.

"See. Arieus'll walk with her," says Tyler as all three guys hold on to their women for dear life.

"Becka, are you cool with that?" asks Jill.

"Yeah I guess it's cool," says Becka hesitantly.

"See, it's cool," says Tyler, joyfully.

"Becka are you sure?" asks Stacey.

"Hell yeah she's sure. Look at the smile on her face," says Tyler.

Becka looks to him, stale faced. "It's cool," she replies as Arieus stands to his feet to walk to the front door.

"Ay Arieus when you come back, if no one answers the door. Just be patient we'll be right out," says Beau.

"And just why won't we be answering the door?" asks Stacey.

Beau whispers in her ear causing her to blush.

"Bye guys," said Becka.

"Call me when you get home," says Jill as Tyler immediately begins to kiss her neck.

"Ok."

"See ya Arieus nice meeting you," says the girls.

Arieus waves good bye as they walk out the door. The apartment complex is filled with cars, not a person in site as Becka speed walks through the parking lot leaving Arieus in her dust.

"You know you don't have to walk me home. I just live up the street. I'll be ok," she says, never turning around.

"Are you sure? Your friends really wanted me to make sure you made it home safely," replies Arieus.

"It's ok. Trust me. I'll be good. You or no one else has to worry about me. I'll be perfectly fine."

"Are you sure?" Arieus asks again.

"Yeah. Positive," she replies, continuing to walk, still never looking back at him.

"Ok," Arieus says turning around.

In his heart he knew this wasn't the right thing to do. But in all actuality he didn't really feel comfortable walking her home in the first place. Little did she know, she was actually doing him a favor.

"So you're really gonna leave?" Becka turns to ask, after only taking a few lonely steps.

"Huh?" Arieus asks, turning around.

"What the hell is wrong with you? Tons of guys would kill to walk me home."

"Huh? I'm only doing what you asked me to do," says Arieus.

"Ok. It's cool. You're right. You don't have to walk me home. You don't owe me anything. I'm just some chick you met tonight. You can go," says Becka before screaming out, "Go!"

"Ok," says Arieus as he turns back around in route to his apartment. He'd recently realized that there was no reason to go back to Lisa's.

"Oh my God. You're still going to walk away," Becka griped, as she and Arieus both turn around yet again. "Why are you treating me like this?" she asks as tears shoot from her eyes. "Come here," she whines, stomping her feet.

Arieus slowly walks over avoiding eye contact.

"Do you think I'm ugly?" she asks, as Arieus steps closer.

"No," replied Arieus, finally looking up at her.

"Yes you do. You have too. You have too," she repeats, as Arieus now stands a few feet away from her. "You haven't said one word to me since you met me. Do you treat all the girls you meet like this?" she asks as she and Arieus are finally face to face.

"No."

"Is it because I'm white? If so, you're fucking stupid. I've been around blacks all my life," she follows.

"It's not that," Arieus says still failing to make eye contact.

146

"Then you must think I'm ugly. Come on just admit it. I'm a big girl. You won't hurt my feelings. Just let it out."

"No. No. I don't," says Arieus.

"So tell me what it is. I wanna know," she demands. "What are you too good for me? Huh? Huh?"

"Too good for you?"

Arieus couldn't believe what she'd said. Obviously she had no clue as to how low his self-esteem was at this point in his life.

"Yeah what else could it be? I'm not stupid. Just be real with me. Tell me what the problem is. I can take it. Go ahead, lay it on me. I'm waiting," she asks, placing her hands to her hips.

Thinking for a second. Arieus pondered on whether or not he should let loose, releasing his true feelings. May sound like an easy task but not for Arieus. This was probably one of the toughest decisions he'd ever made. Still deep inside he knew he'd waited his entire life for moments like this. It didn't take long for him to realize that he had no other options. It was game time. "I don't know how to talk to girls," he confessed.

"What do you mean? How do you talk to other girls? I told you it's because I'm white. I knew it," she declares.

"No. No. It--I--I never had another girl," Arieus explained.

"What do you mean you never had a girl?"

147

"Exactly what I said. I've never had a friend. I've never had anything," said Arieus as his emotions spilled from inside of him in a way he'd never experienced.

"Huh? What are you saying?" Asks Becka, confused.

"I'm saying this is the longest I've ever talked to a girl in my life." Arieus admits before pointing up to the apartments they had just exited. "Tyler, Beaus and Kevin are the only guys who ever talked to me in my life."

"Are you serious?"

"I'm dead serious. I wish I wasn't. But it's true. I got problems you'd never imagine. I just came here to start over."

"Wow. I don't know what to say. You've really never had a girl?" Arieus looks away, fighting back the tears. "So that means you're --"Arieus nods, still avoiding eye contact."And you've never had--?" she asks before stepping closer to Arieus, grabbing him softly by the jaw, slowly turning his face to hers as they leaned in for a kiss. "You've got soft lips," she said smiling up at him.

One thing led to another and the next thing Arieus knew, he was butt naked in the bed of Becka's apartment, more confortable than he'd ever think his first time would be. Becka knew he was a virgin. He had nothing to lose.

Like a veteran she coached him though the ins and outs of making love. As the night progressed he soon felt his cold heart melting. Even in his wildest of dreams he'd never imagined that life could be so sweet. When it was all said and done and they'd both exhausted one another, he laid back, wrapped his arms around his new love before drifting off into his own world, staring up at the ceiling. Only this time there was no blank expression, instead a smile. The smile of a man with not a care in the world.

"**AHHHHHHH**," Arieus said as he sprung up from his sleep kicking and screaming, startling Becka.

"What's wrong?" she asks, startled.

Arieus sat speechless. He'd gotten so caught up in the heat of the moment he'd completely forgotten about his condition. As he slowly looked down to his soaking crotch he contemplated picking up his clothes from the floor and hauling ass.

"It's ok," says Becka soothingly. "You were drinking last night. Shit happens," she says shrugging her shoulders.

Thursday (cont...)

"Ohh shit I can't stop laughing," Pete says struggling to speak. "Ay I can't even lie I wasn't too far from you when I lost my virginity but I'm glad I didn't piss myself after." Pete says continuing his laughter from his bed.

"I'd always been embarrassed about the whole pissing on my self-thing but pissing in front of Becka by far was the worse. I could've died right there."

"But hey on the bright side, besides pissing on yourself it seems to me that college was the shit. Everything you could've asked for. Kinda make me wish I could have went."

"It was. Actually initially it was better than I'd ever expected. I wanted to start a new life but I had no idea it would come so quickly. It was surreal. A brand new confidence had emerged. As I looked into the mirror I didn't even recognize the guy looking back at me. Trust me it was a good thing though."

"Damn that had to feel good," says Pete, smiling. "But on another note what the hell made your ass tell Becka all that shit? How you go from not telling people anything at all about your life to running your whole damn life story down?"

"Man Pete, Becka cried because I was ignoring her. She cried. She cried over something that I did. In my head, only a person who cared about you would do something like that."

"Oh yeah I understand. She was the first person to ever act as if she gave a damn."

"Exactly. I mean, Ray said he cared but let's be honest, the guy was married to my Mom. He was trying to do whatever he had to do to keep his family intact. But Becka, Becka had no reason to care about how I treated her. To me, it just seemed as if she genuinely cared. I can't even explain the feeling."

"True. Yeah I feel you. You only really had one choice in that situation."

"Yeah man. I knew I had to say something. There was no way I could mess that up."

"So did you make her your girl after that?"

"Yeah. I thought she was my soul mate. I thought all my problems were solved, just like the movies."

"Damn and you had your boy Tyler."

"Hell yeah he was the coolest freshman on Campus and I was his roommate. Life couldn't get any better."

"True. But let me ask you something."

"Whatsup."

"What made you go to a White College?"

"What do you mean?"

"After Tim and everybody in his family treating you like shit, what made you still want to go to a white college? I would've thought you would have went to a HBCU or something. Be around your people."

"You know, I've actually never gave it too much thought. Choosing a white college was sorta natural for some reason. As a kid sitting in my room imagining how it must be to be happy, my thoughts were always filled with white faces."

"That's crazy. Well I guess it worked out. Seem like everything was looking up for you."

"Yeah but you know the saying. What goes up must come down."

"Baby, Baby," says Arieus as he taps Becka on the shoulder. She'd fallen asleep in his lap after watching movies on the couch.

"Yes Baby," whispers Becka as she awakens, eyes squinted.

"Baby I'm about to go," says Arieus, sweetly.

Becka looks over to a nearby clock on the wall. It read 9:00. "Why Baby? It's still early."

"I know but you're tired. You've had a long day. I'm gonna let you get some rest. Besides, I forgot my chemistry book and I got a huge test tomorrow."

"But I'm gonna miss you," she pouts as she sits up.

"I'm gonna miss you too baby, "Arieus says as they both stand to their feet. He gently grabs her by the waist bringing her closer. "I'm sorry."

"It's ok," Becka says before exchanging a quick kiss. "I guess it's good for me to have you in my life. Not a lot of guys our age are as mature as you," she adds as Arieus grabs his jacket from the arm of the couch, slipping it on.

"Well thank you baby," Arieus smiles as they both walk up to the front door.

"No. Thank you for being you," says Becka before leaning over for another kiss. This time more passionate.

"See," Arieus says as he shakes his head. "When you kiss me like that you make it so hard for me to leave."

"That's not the only thing that's hard," says Becka as she grabs Arieus crotch.

"Baby," Arieus smiles. "You sure know how to make a man feel good."

They kiss once again before Becka backs away. "Ok baby I'm about to get some rest, college is exhausting," she says.

"Alright babe. I'll call you later to check on you."

"OK baby. Love ya," says Becka as she opens the door.

"Love ya more," follows Arieus as he walks out.

It's only a 15 minute walk from Becka's apartment to Arieus's dorm. Along the way he can't help but to smile, in a matter of months his life had done a complete 360. As he floated through the campus, the brisk winter air collided with his bare face like a sludge hammer, still he was unbothered. The warm embrace of love was all he desired. Life was good.

As he stolled he found himself joking and small talking with different friends and classmates. Simple things he'd always seen others do but had never gotten a chance to do himself. Completely overwhelmed, he decided to do something he'd never done before. Acknowledge God. To him it was only right, after enduring such life changing events, he figured this had to be the work of a higher power. "Thank you Lord," he said to himself as he stepped into his Dormitory.

It's a packed lounge. Male students, study, mingle and watch television as Arieus pleasantly walks up the steps that lead to he and Tyler's room. Just as he's about to turn the knob to enter, Tyler stepped out with Vicki Madison, a young sexy brunette.

"What's up man," says Tyler, before slapping five with Arieus.

"Nothing man. Just about to go in the room and get some studying in."

"Cool that's what me and Vicki just finished doing," replies Tyler, winking at Arieus.

"Is that right." He knew exactly what kind of studying Tyler was referring too. In fact Tyler was known to 'study' more than any guy on campus. "How are you doing Vicki?" asked Arieus.

"Great," she replies with a smile. "You're in my economics class right?"

"Yeah. Mr. Bradford," says Arieus.

"I hate that guy," says Vicki, rolling her eyes.

"Who doesn't," Arieus replies.

"I hate all Professors," follows Tyler as Arieus and Vicki both laugh.

"Trust me, we know," says Arieus as Vicki nods her head.

"Hey at least I'm honest. But I'm about to walk Vicki back to her dorm. I'll be back later bro," says Tyler to Arieus.

"Alright man. See you later Vick. Nice to officially meet you," says Arieus.

"Yeah. I guess I'll see you in old man Bradford's class tomorrow," Vicki follows.

"Don't remind me," says Arieus before walking into room. "Alright guys."

"See ya," says Vicki and Tyler as they walk towards the steps.

After sitting at his desk, studying for hours, Arieus is finally worn out. Unable to fight his exhaustion, he falls asleep face down over his chemistry book before being awaken by a ring on his cell phone. Halfway asleep, he answers. "Hello."

"Where the hell is Tisha?" screams the male voice on the other end.

"Tisha?" asks Arieus. "Sorry sir but I think you might have the wrong number. I don't know anyone by that name."

"I aint got no damn wrong number," says the caller continuing his rant. "I know Tisha's there and I'm going to tell you one time and one time only. You better leave my motherfucking wife alone motherfucker."

"Sir I don't know your wife. I really think you have the wrong number."

"So this aint 543-3245?" the caller asks.

"No. Its 543-3246," replies Arieus.

"Oh. Ok. Damn," he says before hanging up.

Chuckling to himself, Arieus looks over to the clock. It reads 12:22. Realizing he'd never called to check on Becka, he dials her number.

Too bad Becka wasn't really in the mood for talking. She was a little pre occupied at the moment. In nothing but her panties and bra, she comfortably sat on her bed, only to pick up the phone, look at the caller I.D. that read 'My Love' and toss it to the other end of the bed. Completely unaware of the fact that she'd mistakenly pressed the answer button.

"Who was that?" asked Tyler as he walks into her bedroom shirtless.

"Nobody. Just Arieus. All he wants to do is talk about his fucking problems. I mean it was cool at first ya know," says Becka as Tyler sits next to her on the bed. "I guess I was kind of interested in how fucked up someone's life could be. But now it's like….BLAH, BLAH,BLAH," she complains. "Did you know before he came here he never had a single friend?"

"What do you mean?" asks Tyler.

"Exactly what I said. He never had a single friend. Not one. Zip, zilch, nada. I'm the first girl he's ever talked to in his life. Let alone had sex with. The guys a fucking weirdo."

"Damn. I knew he was a little different but I thought it was because it wasn't that many blacks around here."

"No he's just a fucking weirdo, trust me. I had to act like I was asleep tonight just to get him to leave. He's like a little pest. Always up under me," she says as she acts as if she's shaking something off.

Tyler slides closer. "Him being my roommate and all kind of made me like the guy. Hearing you talk about how much he likes you kind of makes me feel guilty about this," says Tyler before Becka leans in throwing her tongue into his mouth.

"Still feel guilty?" she asks, as she seductively backs away.

"On second thought," Tyler says as he sneaks in one more kiss. "I'm sure he'll be ok."

On the other end of the phone Arieus sits trembling, as never before seen veins bulge throughout his face and head as he squeezes the cell phone causing his keypad to nearly pop out.

Hopping to his feet, he frantically searches underneath his bed. After a second, he stands to his feet clutching on to a black back pack.

"Trays Gentleman. Trays," screams Maine.

"Aw come on man, you interrupting us. What you have in the bag bro?" asks Pete as he stands up to look at Arieus.

"Wait until they leave," replies Arieus.

"Wait till they leave? Fuck them," say Pete. "Man just let me know now. This shit getting good as hell. That bitch was a slut. Reminds me of this other girl I heard of," says Pete as he looks over to Eric.

"Hey listen motherfucker. I don't have time for the games. One minute you're crying, wanting to kill yourself. Now you're a comedian. Fuck off," replies Eric, angrily.

"Damn bro. I'm just joking with you. Don't take shit so serious," Pete says as he walks over to the cell bars. "Did I get mad when you told me my girl was in the BIG DICK CLUB? No. I don't care. It's just jokes. Stop letting other people get into your head. You do realize you work in a jail. I can't possibly be the only one who says shit like that. Fuck it."

"He's fucking right Eric. Stop acting like a little bitch," follows Maine.

"You know what. Fuck both of yall," says Eric as Maine slides Pete's tray through the chuck.

"Thanks," says Pete as he grabbed on to his tray. Hot dogs on regular bread, bread putting and string beans.

"Hey Motherfucker are you eating diner today or what?" asks Eric to Arieus as Pete sits on his rack.

"Yeah," replies Arieus.

"What?" says, Maine, surprised. "This the first time your ass done ate all week. I thought you was trying to starve yourself to death."

"It's mind over matter. You only eat because your brain tells you to," says Arieus as he hops down from his rack.

"Hold on. What the fuck is going on? You got this motherfucker talking to us too?" says Maine, directed to Pete.

"Yeah man, he's actually not that bad. He telling me some real shit. And we was just getting to the damn good part before y'all came in here interrupting us with this bullshit y'all call food," Pete says as he stuffs his face.

"Bullshit?" asks Eric as Maine slides Arieus's Tray through. "I can't tell by the way you're chomping it down."

"Thank you," says Arieus as Maine nods.

161

"Nigga aint like I got too much of a choice, this the only food a nigga gonna get, I'm starving in this bitch," says Pete.

"Just use your imagination like when you beat your dick at night," says Eric as Pete flicks him off.

"Well since we're interrupting we'll let you guys get back to whatever it is that you're talking about. I got a nap to get back to anyway," says Maine, yawning.

"Peace out," says Pete as Maine and Eric both walk away.

"Alright so let me know. What the hell was in the bag? Guns?" Asks Pete as he finishes off his string beans.

"I can't lie. This hot dog is pretty good," Arieus says after taking his first bite. "I was fucking starving."

"Yo stop playing. What was in the bag? Did you go kill them niggas? Beat they ass? What you do bro?"

"You know I don't know when the last time I've eaten. I just couldn't get an appetite around here. That's why I just lay here."

"Ok that's cool man. Just tell me what did you go under the bed to get. Did you go over there?" Arieus doesn't answer, only the sound effects of his overly loud chewing can be heard. "Come on man," says Pete before hopping up, looking over to Arieus. "You act like you can't tell the story and eat at the same time. Stop playing."

"Pete. My Brother. Can't I at least enjoy my meal?"

"Nigga this jail. Meals aint meant to be enjoyed. They meant to keep us alive. Throw that shit back and move on. Now what the hell happened bro? What the hell was in the book bag? You can't just stop at a part like that. I need to know." Pete demanded.

"You gon eat your cornbread?" Arieus asks.

"Nigga," Pete shouts.

"I'm just joking. It's a joke. You never seen Martin Lawrence and Eddie Murphy's movie 'Life'? Can't I crack a joke every once in a while."

"Yeah man. Crack all the jokes you want," says Pete. "Ha-ha very funny. Now just come on with the story."

"Ok. Ok. Well as you know I've had trust issues in my life. So even though life was going great. I still had that 'What if' mind state. So with that being said. I always kept a bag full of everything from my gun, to duct tape and handcuffs. Just in case something needed to be done. And what do you know. Something needed to be done."

2004

"Oh baby," moans Becka as Tyler licks her naked breast, slowly making his way down. Only to be interrupted by a knock at the door.

"Who the fuck is that?" whispers Tyler before Becka motions for him to be quiet.

"I don't know," answers Becka as the knocks proceed. Pushing Tyler off, she quietly steps out of bed, grabbing her robe, creeping to the front door. Gazing through the peep hole, she discovers, its Arieus. "Shit," she whispers to herself. He stands, not appearing mad, instead he's smiling. "Oh shit," Becka whispers once again before tip toeing back into the bedroom.

"Who is it?" asks Tyler, standing naked.

"Arieus," she says as the knocks proceed and the phone rings, echoing through the quiet house. There was no way she would be able to say she didn't hear it.

"What is he doing here?" Tyler asks as he searches for his clothes.

"I don't know. He never pops up," she follows.

"What the hell are we going to do?" asks Tyler as Arieus continues to knock.

"Go hide in there. I'm going to get him out of here," says Becka, pointing over to the small closet behind her.

"Hide in the closet?" Tyler asks.

"Yeah. It'll be quick" she insures.

"Ok," says Tyler, reluctantly, making his way over after slipping on his paints and shirt before picking up his shoes.

"One second," says Becka to Arieus. Before walking to the living room. "Who is it?" she asks.

"It's me Baby," says Arieus calmly.

Slightly cracking the door, Becka squints her eyes, attempting to give the illusion that she'd been fast asleep. "Hey Baby. What are you doing over here so late? I was passed out," she says.

For a brief second Arieus continues smiling before his expression quickly turned into a menacing stare. In the blink of an eye he grabbed Becka by the neck with his right hand, covering her mouth with the left. Both hands covered by black leather gloves.

Bursting through the door he forcefully turns her body around until she's facing the same directions as him. With his hand remaining over her mouth, he whips his gun from his waiste before thrusting it

165

into her side. "Don't say a word," he whispers into her ear as he kicks the door shuts, slowly guiding her to the bedroom.

Entering the room, Arieus again whispers into Becka's ear. "I'm about to push you onto the bed. Once I do, don't make a sound. If you do, I will kill the both of you. Do you hear me?" he asks slowly as Becka nods her head. "Good," he says before pushing her onto the bed.

As she lay face down sobbing onto her comforter Arieus removes his book bag from his back before carefully searching through, pulling out a pair of handcuffs and duct tape as he tosses the bag onto the bed. Aggressively grabbing both of her wrist, he locks them together. "Is he in the closet?" he whispers as he leans down to her ear.

Fearing for her life, Becka nods yet again as Arieus rips off a small piece of Duct tape, slapping it onto her lips. Picking his back pack up from the bed, he drops the tape back inside. "Remember, make one sound and you're dead," he whispers as she nods yet again as he creeps over to the closet door.

Swinging it open, he instantly points the pistol directly at Tyler's face before he can utter a word. "Follow me. Make one sound or try to run and it's over for you and our little bitch."

"Ok. I'm Sorr-" he attempts to say.

"Shut up," says Arieus in a low, commanding tone as he grabs Tyler by the belt buckle placing the gun to his side. Together they walk towards the front door. "So you just couldn't stick to fucking everyone else's girl around campus. You just had to fuck mine didn't you," he says, continuing to whisper.

"Dude it's not--," Tyler attempts to explain.

"Motherfucker didn't I tell your bitch ass to shut the fuck up," says Arieus as he shoves the pistol harder into Tyler's side.

"Sor--," Tyler starts to say before stopping his own self.

"Walk to your car."

Tyler's body shakes and trembles. Not only out of fear but because of the night air. Uncaring, Arieus, surveys the parking lot. No one is around.

"Oh I get it," Arieus says as they approach the vehicle. "You tried to park far away from her apartment just in case I popped up I wouldn't see your car. Smart, but not smart enough. Give me your fucking keys," Arieus says as he digs his hands into Tyler's pocket. "All of this could have been avoided but look what you made me do," Arieus says as he reaches his destination. "Just look," says, Arieus strongly as he pops the trunk.

Tyler looks back. He starts to mouth the words 'I'm sorry' but quickly realizes that may not be the right thing to do as Arieus stares soulless into his eyes.

"Don't move."

Hesitantly, Tyler obliges.

Never removing the gun from his side, dropping the bag to the ground, Arieus crouches down, now pointing the gun up to Tyler as he opens the bag reaching inside, pulling out even more Duct tape and another set of cuffs. "Give me your hands," Arieus urges as he rises to his feet, after laying the duct tape on the ground.

Pointing the gun to Tyler's side, he multitasks with his other hand, grabbing him by the wrists placing them to the front, and slapping on the cuffs. "Remember, make one sound and you're a dead man," says Arieus as he reaches down for the tape, ripping off a piece with his teeth before dropping the rest. Remembering where he was, he looks around once again to ensure no one was watching. Again he was safe as he through the tape over Tyler's mouth.

Dropping his pistol to the side, he speaks, "Get your ass in that trunk," he says before pushing Tyler inside and immediately closing it.

After scoping out the parking lot Arieus storms back up to the apartment. His heart thumps as he reentered the crib, discovering Becka still lying flat in the same position he'd left her, face drenched with tears.

"Hey baby," he says before searching through her closet, pulling out a small black dress. "I've always loved this dress.

Remember you wore it to our date to the Opera last month. You looked so good. You didn't even wear any panties. You let me finger you the whole show. Thank God for that back row. I thought you were all mine. The way you looked at me," Arieus says as he massages Becka's back. "The way that pussy got wet for me," he says as he places his hands between her thighs, reminiscing. "I'm such a fool. I really believed you when you said I was the only one who got you to that point. Turns out you were full of shit. Makes me wonder just what else you were lying about, Becka, if that's even your real name," he says before removing his hands from her body.

"I'm going to uncuff you and you're going to throw this dress on. I just want to see you wear it one last time. Maybe it'll remind me of the good days and I won't have to hurt you," he says as he uncuffs her. Backing up, he raises his gun, pointing it to her chest. "Man you look good," he says as she stands to her feet, looking to the floor as she dressed. "Don't even have to wear a bra. Breast just firm and perky. You look stunning," he admits. "I thought you were perfect," says Arieus as Becka's tears splash onto the floor. "No need to cry now baby. Your little boy toy is dead. Now I'm going to take this duct tape off of your mouth, it might hurt a little. But hey, we both know you enjoy a little pain," he says.

"Oh my God," Becka whines as he snatches the tape away.

"Bitch didn't I say don't make a sound," says Arieus as he places the gun onto Becka's head as she nods, frightened. "Now

169

move," he says lowering the gun to her waist as they walk side by side out of the apartment in route to Tyler's Car.

Becka's teeth chatter and body shiverered the entire walk over to the vehicle. Before entering Arieus slaps the handcuffs back onto her wrist and shoves her into the back seat, gently shutting the door. Next he throws his back pack into the passenger seat and enters the car from the driver's side before pulling out of the parking lot.

Looking back at Becka he smiles, winking.. "Hey baby," he says before reaching over to his back pack, pulling out a disk and sliding it into the car's CD player.

"*Meet me at the Crossroads*," Arieus sings as Bone Thugs n Harmony's hit song 'Crossroads' blasts through the stereo system. He raps along as he stares at Becka's teary eyed face through the rearview mirror. *'And I'm gonna miss everybody, And I'm gonna miss everybody'* he raps loudly.

The song repeats itself about five times before the trio finally arrive to 'Ships Pier' an old boat dock no one frequented anymore. Once upon a time it was a pretty popular hangout but after a few women said they'd been raped and left for dead by some masked maniac, its reputation sort of went down the drain, leaving it all but abandoned for years.

Still humming, 'Crossroads', Arieus emerges from the car before violently dragging Becka out by her feet. Picking her up by her neck, he places her in a choke hold before walking her over to the

170

trunk. Popping it open, he screams, "Surprise," as Tyler is revealed, still alive. "See, I'm not such a bad guy after all. I didn't even kill him. You happy? Huh?" Arieus asks Becka, before smacking her on the ass while she stood silently. "Aw shit, I forgot I told you not to make a sound. You're smart," he says as he kisses her cheek, right arm still wrapped around her neck. "Actually the both of you are. Just not smart enough," Arieus says as he places his gun on his hip, grabbing Tyler by the feet with his left hand, dragging him out of the trunk as he falls hard to the ground.

Arieus stands over top of him smiling as Tyler's frightened eyes look up to him. "Whats up Tyler," Arieus says before speaking to Becka. "I bet you're used to seeing him from this angle. I know how much you love to be on top. Only this time you're not in control. I am," he says before giving Becka one more kiss on the cheek. "It's getting kinda boring talking to myself. I guess I can let you say something Becka," he says looking down at Tyler. "I would say you could talk also but then I'd have to reach down and take off the tape while still holding Becka. Just a lot of unnecessary bullshit. Plus I know what you're gonna say. 'I'm sorry. Blah Blah Blah' When the truth is I really don't give a damn what you say. But Becka, I am kinda curious as to what you have to say. So I'm going to ask you one more time. Why?" Arieus asks still looking down to Tyler.

"I --," says Becka.

"Bitch I was lying," Arieus interrupts. "I don't really want your whore ass to talk." He says before kissing Becka once more.

171

"I'm just joking, Just a joke. You can talk. Hey, maybe that's the problem. Maybe I didn't joke enough. Maybe I should have been a funny guy like Tyler. Maybe then I could have stopped you from being a little whore. You think that would have worked?"

Becka stands silent, unsure of what to do or say.

"It's ok. You can talk. I'm being honest," says Arieus. "Come on, let it out."

Hesitantly Becka speaks. "It wasn't you. It was me."

"It wasn't you it was me," Arieus repeats, mockingly. "The oldest line in the book. A gun up in your face and that's all that you can come up with? Are you fucking serious?" he asks, chuckling, before looking down at Tyler. "Is she kidding me?"

"I'm being honest. You're a great guy. It's me. I'm the one who betrayed your trust," Becka continues, as Tyler remains still, looking up at the two.

"Yes. Yes you did," Arieus agrees.

"And I really am sorry. But hurting us isn't going to fix anything."

"Aw man. You had me until you said that bullshit. That's where you're wrong sweetie. Hurting you will definitely fix a lot. But honestly when did anyone say anything about hurting you?"

"I mean you have us handcuffed at the pier," she follows.

172

"Yeah you're right. I'd probably think the same thing. But actually you're wrong. You know how?"

"How?" she asks reluctantly.

"I'm not going to hurt you silly. Nor am I going to hurt ol Tyler over here. I swear," Arieus says as he kisses Becka yet again. "Seriously. Trust me. Do you trust me?"

After releasing a sigh of relief Becka responds. "Yes."

"Good, at least one of us is trustworthy," Arieus says, continuing to shower her with kisses. "Man I love the way you taste," he says after licking her face, switching his attention down to Tyler, staring him deep in the eyes as he continued his conversation with Becka. "Ok I got one more question. You wanna hear it baby?"

"Yes."

"Do you love me?"

"Yes. I really do. You're the best guy I've ever met."

Arieus smiles, "So you really think we can work?"

"Yes. I know we can."

"And you're never gonna do anything like this again?"

"No. I swear. I won't. Just give me another chance," Becka pleads.

"So you're telling me that after all this. Me bringing you to the pier, handcuffing you, you'd still give me another shot? Is that what you're telling me?" asks Arieus.

"Yes, Arieus you just gotta believe me. I swear. I love you baby. I really am sorry from the bottom of my heart. This will never and I mean never in a million years happen again. Everyone makes mistakes," replies Becka, sounding sincere.

"You're right everyone does. I know you're sorry baby. I believe you. You don't know how much better you've just made me feel. But unfortunately. It's not you who I don't trust. Its him," says Arieus, still looking down to Tyler. "He doesn't know how to keep his dick in his pants. Did you know he just had gonorrhea last month? Gono-fucking-rhea. Come on baby. You really gotta be more careful. Can't just be fucking every little cute blonde haired motherfucker that comes around. You understand?" asks Arieus as he slightly tightens his grip around Becka's neck.

"I know baby. I'll never do it again. I swear."

"I believe you baby. But he needs to learn a lesson. He can't just go on thinking he can stick that nasty little thing in everything he wants. You agree?"

Hesitantly Becka says, "Yes." During this whole ordeal, she hadn't once looked down to Tyler. Can't say the same for him though, scared for his life, anytime Arieus looked away for a split second, his

174

eyes shot up to Becka, hoping they can maybe lock eyes and somehow come up with a plan to save their young life's.

"Baby, I'm so glad you agree with me," replies Arieus. That's why I'm going to let you do the honors. He says before grabbing a knife from his front pocket. "Now," Arieus speaks slowly. "I'm going to take these handcuffs off of you and I want you to take his pants off. I'm pretty sure you know how to do that. Ok."

"Ok," she follows.

"And after you take his pants off I want you to take his boxers off. Wait never mind, I remember him saying he doesn't wear underwear. Easy access. Remember that?" says Arieus to Tyler as Tyler looks timidly up at him. "Oh shit, that's what it is, you two probably bonded over the fact that neither of you like to wear underwear. I get it, I get it. But anyway, back to the topic at hand. I want you to pull his pants down, take this knife I'm going to give you and cut that little snake of a penis he has right off." Tyler's eye bulge as Becka's body continues to shake. "You think you can handle that baby?"

"Are you sure?" asks Becka in a low tone.

"Am I fucking sure? Am I fucking sure?" Arieus screams. "Do you see where the fuck you at?" he continues, forcing Becka to look around. "Huh bitch? Do I look like I'm not sure about anything that's going on? Yes I'm fucking sure. Now again. Do you think you can handle that baby?" he asks, lowering his tone.

Closing her eyes taking in a deep breath, Becka quietly replies, "Yes."

"Good," Arieus says as he releases her from the choke hold, uncuffing her and placing the knife into her hands.

He steps to the side while pointing the gun to her.

Looking back to Arieus one last time, it doesn't take long for Becka to realize he was serious. Taking in a deep breath, she slowly bends to her knees. For the first time she and Tyler lock eyes. Holding on to his small glimmer of hope, Tyler never looks away.

"Take his pants off," Arieus barks, shutting down their mini reunion as he continued pointing the gun.

"Ok," Becka follows before unbuttoning Tyler's pants, pulling them down to his mid-thigh.

"Wow," Arieus says, chuckling. "I'll just assume the cold air is making your dick so little. But hey at least you're wearing a condom this time. Now cut that dirty motherfucker off," he says as Becka looks back to him as she swallows a mountain of spit. "Do it," he urges. "Cut that motherfucker off. Now," shouts Arieus stepping closer, placing the gun next to Becka's head. "Now," he yells, louder.

"Ok. Ok," she says, grabbing a hold of Tyler's small flaccid Penis as his eyes bulge.

"Do it now," Arieus demands.

Tears continue to fall as Becka mouths the words 'I'm sorry' to Tyler before turning her head to the side, chopping away from the root as his agonizing screams are muffled by the duct tape still placed tightly around his mouth.

Blood squirts and leaks, covering both Tyler's crotch and stomach as well as Becka's hand. His face turns blue as his head appears to be seconds away from exploding. Unable to control himself he squirms away, backing up causing Arieus to grow enraged.

"Stop," Arieus bolts as he walks over to Tyler who appears half dead, head hanging loosely off of his shoulders like a puppet. "You aint gonna run away from this motherfucker," says Arieus as he takes one cuff off of Tyler, dragging his weak body to the driver's side door as he continues to moan in pain. After handcuffing Tyler's right wrist to the door handle, Arieus looks over to Becka and her blood soaked hand. "Continue."

Struggling to gain her composure Becka breathes heavily as she slowly made her way over to Tyler. Dropping to her knees, she picks up where she'd left off seconds ago.

"Yeah just like that. Cut that motherfucker," Arieus cheers, still pointing the gun to her. Incapable of bearing the pain Tyler passes out, leaving his body shaking and convulsing, hanging from the door handle similar to his penis, limp.

"You did a great job baby," Arieus says as Becka finally completes her mission, dropping Tylers dismembered penis onto the

177

ground. "But I thought that would make me feel better. Turns out, it didn't. Actually I think I'm going to need him dead. I thought I could handle it but I cant. Sorry. Slice his ass," he shouts, somehow awakening Tyler as his eyes bulge and he vehimately shakes his head, silently pleading for his life.

"No. Arieus. No. Please. I can't," whines Becka.

"You mean to tell me you want him alive that bad you'd try to save his life. Even though it could cost us our relationship?" he asks as he raises his gun back towards her.

"No baby, I," she stutters. "It's not for him. It's for me. I don't know if I can live with the fact that I took someone's life. You gotta understand," she adds, stuttering, losing control of her words.

"Bitch I aint gotta understand shit. You made your bed now lay in it," he demands. "Now I'm going to say this one more time. Slice his ass. Now," he screams, pointing the gun to the back of her head.

"Ok. Ok.," she says.

"Now," Arieus screams.

Closing her eyes, Becka raises the knife before stabbing Tyler continuously throughout his body.

"Yeah. Just like that. Keep going," urges Arieus as Becka stabs hole after hole as thick red blood sqirts covering her from her face to her knees.

At the same time Becka cries uncontrollably before Arieus gives permission to seize. "You may stop," says Arieus, as Becka fails to control her sobbing. "Good job."

No question, Tyler is dead. His blood coated, lifeless body lays motionless on the ground as his arm and wrist remain propped up by the now red stained door handle.

"Was that so hard?" Arieus asks as Becka continues crying, ignoring Arieus question. "I said was that so hard?" he asks again.

"No," she replies hardly able to release her words.

She sits, delusional, staring away from Tyler's body.

"I bet. See, I wish it didn't have to be like this. You guys were the coolest people I'd ever met. But you betrayed me. This was my only choice," he says before walking over to Becka leaning over to her blood speckled forehead as her body tensed. "Do you still love me baby?" he asks.

Taking her time, she responds, "Ye--"

Times up. Too long. Arieus's patience had grown thin. In the blink of an eye he ferousiously threw her into a sleeper hold, choking life from her.

"Why you lying to me bitch you don't love me. You don't fucking love me. You never did. You never fucking did," he screams, as he squeezes tighter and tighter around her neck.

"Arieus, I can't--."

She attempts to speak but Arieuss' strength was far too much for her, within seconds she was passed out.

Dropping her body to the ground, Arieus grabs her right hand, positioning it onto the gun as if she was taking her own life. Placing the cold steel weapon to her temple, he pulls the trigger.

"Bitch," he whispers as the bullet shatters her skull releasing everything that dwelled inside, leaving her lying dead, spread across the ground.

Finally he uncuffs Tyler, snatching the tape from around his mouth as his entire body drops to the ground side by side with Becka. Once again smiling, he reaches into his pockets for Tyler's car keys before a light bulb pops in his head.

Bending over, he retrieves Tyler's dismembered penis from off the ground before stuffing it into Becka's mouth. "Whore," he says before calmly strolling away into the night.

Thursday (cont...)

"About two days later I was woken up by Officers at my front door," says Arieus, staring, nonchalantly at the ceiling.

"Hold on don't tell me you got arrested," Pete, says still lying down. "When they locked my ass up they made sure they told the whole world every little thing I'd done in the past. But I see they left out your criminal history. That's crazy."

"Actually you're wrong. I never said I was arrested. Just questioned. Too bad there was no evidence. No one saw me. It wasn't like I left any of my blood or anything laying around. I was smart, I tossed everything I had on that night into a lake across town along with the cuffs, duct tape, gloves and gun."

"At least somebody learned something from watching all them crime shows. But hold on why the hell did they come and question you in the first place?"

"It turns out I was the last to find out about the whole Tyler and Becka affair. So naturally everyone kinda figured I had something to do with it. Only thing was, they couldn't prove it," replies Arieus.

"So that was your second murder. Well second and third. Boy, let me find out you some sort of serial killer or something. I thought you was just out here killing little black boys I aint know you was killing everybody," Pete says laughing. "You a bad motherfucker."

"I felt I had no choice. I'd been mistreated so much in life there was no way I could let someone continue to do blatantly disrespect me with no consequences. As crazy as it may sound. My conscience wouldn't allow me to. "

"So again you mean to tell me you aint have no remorse at all. You was completely fine with the shit you did?

"After that happened, it sort of gave me a new outlook on life."

"How?"

"It made me realize that the whole dream world that I had imagined all my life was false. The shit didn't exist. It actually taught me one of the greatest lessons I could ever learn."

"What's that?"

"Trust no one," he says evilly. "I grew up thinking that I was trapped in a small world that didn't love me. But after that situation I learned that, that's just how the world was. Love didn't exist. It was only an imaginary word people through around in order to benefit themselves."

"I don't know bro. I love people and I'm pretty sure there are some people who love me back," Pete follows.

"Yeah and that might be true. Maybe I am taking it to the extreme. But there is no way you can really tell if a person truly loves you. It's impossible."

"I can tell by their actions."

"You think you can. And that's exactly what they want you to do. The whole time they have ulterior motives that you're completely unaware of. Just think about the guy who put you in Prison. You thought he really cared for you didn't you?"

"Damn you got a point," says Pete, nodding his head.

"I bet he showed you in every way that he really loved you didn't he?"

"Yep."

"Then just when you thought he was genuine and that you had no worries when it came down to him, he sat on that bench and basically murdered you broad day light."

"Hell yeah. You fucking right," Pete says, disappointingly shaking his head.

"See what I mean?"

"Yeah I see what you mean. I just can't let myself think like that. Like I said it's gotta be some good people in this world besides myself."

"You're right. But like I just said, how would you know when it's truly genuine or not."

"I don't know," answers Pete.

"Exactly. That's why I chose not to believe in love at all."

"True. I can understand that. Alright, so after all that went down you just stayed in school? Didn't it feel funny considering what had went down?"

"I tried to continue school but I kinda lost my drive. Not to mention everyone thought I was a murderer. But it was OK. I had figured out a new career."

"The motherfucking police."

"Yep. While the Police were questioning I realized that they had 90 percent control over their own destiny. The only other time I truly thought I had control over a situation was when I had weapons in my hand. But as a Cop, not only would I always get to carry my weapon but I'd have the power to display my control over people at any time I chose."

"So you said fuck school."

"Yep. Fuck it. Packed up and moved to Norfolk, Va. It was payback time."

2015

It's the middle of the afternoon and Arieus along with his partner Ed, a young upbeat white cop walk towards a small four door Honda Accord Arieus had just pulled over. Although the day had barely began, this was by far the duo's first stop. Hell no, Arieus had grown Notorious in the city of Norfolk for being Officer 'Constipation', he didn't let shit slide.

"How you doing Ma'am?" asks Arieus.

"Fine Officer," answers Martha Simpson, a middle aged pleasant black woman. "Just on my way home from the Dr.. How are you?"

"I'm fine," replies Arieus. "Are you aware of why I pulled you over today?"

"No officer I'm afraid I'm not," she answers.

"Well, do you by chance see that sign placed right over there?" he asks pointing to the speed indicator just a few feet away from them.

"Yes, I do," she says looking over to the road sign.

"What does it say?" asks Arieus.

Squinting her eyes to read, Martha replies, "It says Speed Limit 35."

"And are you aware of just how fast my partner and I clocked you at?" Arieus questions as he points back to Ed.

"No sir but I'm sure it could not have been too much over. I always go the speed limit. Always," she responds.

"Well I'm afraid that isn't true. We clocked you at 39 miles per hour," says Arieus, matter of a factly.

"39?" she asks with a smirk. "Yes but that's only 4 miles over."

"Right. But again ma'am. Do you see what that sign reads?" asks Arieus pointing over once again.

"Yes but--."

"Sorry," Arieus interrupts. "I don't want to hear any buts. Rules are rules."

"I don't mean any disrespect officer but 4 miles seems a tad bit petty doesn't it?"

"Ma'am excuse my French but I don't give a damn if its 1 mile over. Rules are rules like I said. If we wanted you to go 39 than that would be the speed limit. But it's not. Is it?"

"But--"

"But nothing," Arieus arrogantly interrupts once again. "Now do you have your license and registration?"

"Yes," Martha says, rolling her eyes. "I do," she follows as she retrieves the I.D. from her purse and the registration out of her glove compartment. "Here," she speaks with an attitude as she handed the documents over.

"Thank you. I'll be right back," says Arieus before walking back to his squad car as Ed follows behind. He shrugs and smiles at the lady as if somehow trying to ensure her that he had nothing to do with her treatment. This isn't the first time he hasn't fully agreed with Arieus's practices. But by now Arieus wasn't the same low self-esteem, head hanging low loser he once was.

Nor was he the same happy go lucky, gentle guy he was back in college. Things had long changed. After earning his badge his confidence sky-rocketed through the roof. It was his way or the highway. Ed was no match for the new no-non-sense Arieus. He had a way of calling shots and demanding respect without so much as saying a word. One might even say that Ed was afraid of him.

Actually maybe he wasn't afraid. It's just that there really wasn't much he could do at the time. Since they'd become partners it wasn't like Arieus hadn't always played by the rules. Foul play was never part of his agenda. Yeah he may have been a little harsh, borderline crazy but still technically there was nothing Ed could say about it. So most often he simply sat there, silent, looking stupid.

Arieus was Batman and he was Robin. Who would have ever seen a thing like that coming?

Just a few miles down the road four teen aged black boys are taking part in a few real crimes. They sit, chilling in a stolen Camaro in front of a small one story home in Huntersville, a lower class neighborhood in Norfolk. In recent months the entire city had pretty much turned into a death zone making it the most dangerous city's in all of Virginia.

Roddy Lawson, a small 17 year old boy sits in the passenger seat as Chima Harper a 14 year old baby faced kid sits behind him in the back along with the more mature appearing 16 year old Ricci White, who sits texting on his phone.

The ring leader of the bunch, 16 year old Bobby Hall, sits comfortably in the driver's seat.

"Yo. Why the fuck we gotta sit in front of my crib?" asks Roddy directed to Bobby.

"You want the weed don't you?" replies Bobby.

"Yeah," answers Roddy.

"Well this is where he told me to meet him at. What you complaining about?"

188

"What am I complaining about?" asks Roddy. "Nigga you act like you couldn't've told him to come somewhere else. My Mama can come home any minute," he says looking back, paranoid.

"So. We just sitting in the damn car. Fuck is the problem?" asks Bobby, shrugging his shoulders.

"Fuck is the problem? Nigga is you high already?" shouts Rod. "This aint no regular damn car, this shit stolen. Did you forget or something?"

"I aint forget shit," Bobby says remaining calm. "Nigga how the fuck your mama gon know it's stolen?"

"Bruh I aint talking about my Mama knowing it's stolen. I'm talking about the Police pulling up on us and we get arrested right in front of her crib. You know my mama don't like being embarrassed, and me getting arrested in front of all these damn neighbors is embarrassing. She gon beat my ass," Roddy whines.

The nigga wasn't lying. Wonda, his Mother, was a tad bit different than a lot of the parents in the hood. Of course no one wants there child in the street acting like a wild animal, it's just that in a lot of situations after kids repeatedly get into trouble week after week, parents tend to wash their hands. For most they already have other kids to worry about not to mention their own stresses. This wasn't the case with Wonda, she was willing to do any and everything in her power to keep her baby alive and out of the possession of the state.

Roddy was her only child, all she had in the world. Being a single mom, she didn't have all of the answers on how to raise a black boy in the hood but she figured beating his ass was always a good option. Even with Roddy being 17, Wonda was still known to come outside in the middle of the night after he'd missed his curfew, head full of rollers, hands gripping a leather beltt, ready to teach her disobedient offspring a lesson. She didn't give a damn. With every

whipping she hoped she somehow knocked some sense into her boy.

Not too sure if it was working, peer pressure is a motherfucker. Living in a hood like Huntersville he couldn't help but to get into a little mischief every now and then. Trouble was like 7-eleven, it was on every corner. To him, his only option was to make sure he stayed as under the radar as possible. But with a best friend like Bobby it was damn near impossible.

Bobby was the type of kid who got a kick out of chasing the thrill of danger. Time and time again he always seemed to be involved in something off the wall, something that would get the whole hood talking. He loved the attention.

Of course Wonda hated it and with her ears always planted to the streets, she more often than not found out. Infact there were times she'd gone so far as to ban Roddy from hanging with Bobby. Still, it never worked, Bobby was a handsome sweet heart, with a twinkle in his eyes that forced forgiveness on whoever he wronged.

"Yo chill the fuck out. I changed the license plates. Even if the police come they aint even gonna know it was stolen. You trippin bro," fires back Bobby.

"Yeah you trippin bro," adds Chima.

"Yo aint nobody ask you shit. I'm getting tired of you always co-signing Bobby. You act like he your damn Daddy or something," Roddy replies, looking back to Chima.

"Chill bro. Leave him alone. If you don't want him to meet us here, hear," Bobby says as he passes Roddy his cell phone. "Call him and tell him to meet us somewhere else."

"Hell naw. You call him," says Rod pushing the phone from away from him.

"Nigga why would I call him? I'm not the one who wanna leave . You is."

"Yeah but that nigga crazy I aint bouta tell that nigga to change his plans. What if he already on his way over here."

"You a pussy," says Bobby causing Chima to burst into laughter.

"Yo why the fuck you always laughing?" Roddy screams to Chima as he turns his body around in the seat to face him once again. "Yo Bobby get your little nigga before I beat his ass. No bullshit. I aint playing no more," he says, switching his attention over to Bobby.

"Nigga why you always saying something to me but not Bobby. What you scared of him or something?" replies back Chima.

"What nigga?" Roddy asks, turning back around.

"You heard me nigga," Chima, replies as they stare off at one another. "You scared of Bobby?"

"Yo both of yalll chill," Bobby demands.

Roddy follows the orders, turning around, upset as his body rocked back and forth in the seat. He had no come back for Chima. In his heart he knew he was right, he was afraid of Bobby. Who wasn't? Although he wasn't a big guy, Bobby was known as the 'Knockout King', he had a one hitter quitter that could send the biggest of men plummeting to the ground. And in that special case where someone would actually get the best of him, everyone always knew, without a shadow of a doubt he was coming back for more. Again and again, until victory was his. Giving up wasn't even in his vocabulary.

Knowing this, it sorta put a battery in Chima's back, he always knew, if his mouth ever got him into something he couldn't handle, he could always count on his big cousin Bobby to have his back. This especially bothered Roddy. It's not that he didn't like Chima It's just that he was annoying as hell.

Still, at the end of the day they were still all friends. Hung out daily and for the most part, had fun. Yeah they argued a lot but it was always easy for something to take their attention off of the bickering.

Right now, it was Korb SKii. He was the crew's favorite rapper and his hit song 'Feeling Myself' had just came blaring through the radio.

"Ayyye this my shit," says Chima.

"Hell yeah. Turn that shit up bro," follows Roddy.

Bobby follows the request as everyone goes crazy, singing along to every word.

Except for Ricci. Instead, he stares into his phone. If you've noticed he hasn't said a word. He and his girlfriend Deja are in the middle of one of their usual arguments. "What," he mumbles as he reads a text that stated, "All you ever want to do is hang out with your friends. What about me? You're so dumb.'

"Dumb?" he says loudly to himself, catching Chima's attention.

"Huh?" asks Chima, looking over to Ricci. "Dump? You gotta take a dump," Chima asks over the loud music as Ricci ignores him, hopping out the car.

As the song comes to an end Bobby turns the radio down. "Yo that's the shit," he says.

"Damn right. That's that new Korb Skii. His whole mixtape go hard," follows Roddy, still bobbing his head.

"Hottest of the year. No funny shit," shoots back Bobby.

They give each other high fives.

"You aint never lied," adds Roddy. "Yo man, where the hell is Tony?"

"He's coming man," answers Bobby.

"And where the hell is Ricci?" asks Roddy after turning to look in the backseat.

"Yeah. Where the hell is Ricc?" Bobby says looking back.

"I think he said something was dumb or either he had to take a dump. I don't know," replies Chima.

Roddy quickly looks back, "Take a dump? Where?'"

"Yeah man I think that what he said. The music was too loud I couldn't really hear him. I asked him what he said but he just jetted out."

"Hold on. Hold on," Roddy says looking out his window. "I don't see that nigga. You mean to tell me that niggas dumping in my backyard or something?" he asks, looking back to Chima, who shrugs. "Yo I swear I'ma beat his ass if he dumping outside my house."

"Yo if you gotta go you gotta go," says Bobby as he and Chima laugh hysterically.

"Fuck that! If my Mom pull up and he's dumping, she's gonna kill me. I'm about to go get that nigga," says Rod before Bobby turns around looking out the back window, causing Chima and Rod to look back also.

"Who the hell is that?" asks Bobby.

"Man I hope it aint my Mom," replies Roddy

"Nope I think that's Tony," says Chima.

"It better be," says Rod.

"It is," Bobby confirms. "Just chill," he adds as the car parks directly behind them. "Wait till I get back to find Ricci, both of us don't need to get out the car, it might draw too much attention and you know how nosey your neighbors can get."

"Ok. But I swear if that nigga dumping in my yard, I'm beating his fucking ass, no question. Fuck that."

Outside, Ricci who had decided to take a walk while on the phone, is on his way back to the vehicle. "I'm sorry baby I don't know how I forgot we were going out tonight. I promise Ima make it up," he whines over the phone to Deja.

"That's what you said last week. Call me when you grow up," she says, full of attitude.

"Baby--" says Ricci before realizing he was too late and that she'd already hung up. "Man," he says as he heads back to the car, noticing that Tony is parked behind him. He nods over to him before

195

entering back into the stolen vehicle as Bobby quickly exits. "Yo yall know that's Tony right there behind us?"

"Yeah nigga," Roddy says instantly turning around to him. "Didn't you just see Bobby get out the car?"

"Nigga who the fuck you think you talking to like that?" asks Ricci.

"Nigga, I'm talking to you. What the fuck was you doing out there?" asks Roddy.

"What you mean what was I doing? I was minding my own damn business," shoots back Ricci.

"Fuck is that supposed to mean?" replies Roddy.

"Nigga exactly what I said. I was minding my own damn business. It aint got shit to do with you."

"Aint got nothing to do with me? Nigga, did you take a dump in my yard?"

"What?" Ricci shouts, surprised.

"Nigga you heard me. Did you take a dump in my back yard?"

"Hell naw I aint take no dump in your yard."

"Well nigga let me be clear. Did you take a dump on the side of my yard, or anywhere near my yard?"

"Nigga what? I'm not answering no dumb shit like that."

"What nigga?" asks Roddy, angrily. "You better answer me. Did you or didn't you. I'm tryna save you from an ass whipping."

"Ass whipping? Nigga you better stop talking to me like you some gangsta or something. Fuck you think you is?"

"Nigga," Roddy replies before speaking slowly. " Did you take a dump or not? I aint gon ask no more."

"You aint gon ask no more? Do you hear this nigga?" asks Ricci looking over to Chima who nods his head, enjoying the entertainment.

"Yeah nigga you heard me. I aint gonna ask no more," says Roddy as he and Ricci, eye tussle.

"Well yeah nigga. I took a dump. I dumped everywhere and wiped my ass with the water bill bitch," Ricci Shouts.

Roddy instantly jumps to the back seat.

"You took a damn dump in my yard," he yells as he swings and misses. Ricci then grabs Roddy and they commence to wrestling.

"Chill, Chill," shouts, Chima, as he struggles to hold in his laughter. This is far from unusual, tussles like this happen on a daily basis.

"Yo, yo," Bobby screams as he reenters the car, yanking Roddy back to the front seat. "Yo what the fuck is yall doing?"

"Bitch ass nigga really was back there dumpin in my damn yard," Roddy says still looking back at Ricci.

"Fuck you nigga. Who the fuck you think you calling a bitch? Wont nobody dumping in your damn yard."

"Well why the fuck you say you was then nigga? I don't got time for games. I aint no fucking PlayStation."

"Nigga fuck you. Your ass the one who kept telling me I did, I just gave you what you obviously wanted to hear."

"Yo shut the fuck up," demands Bobby. "Yall niggas both sound retarded."

"Hell yeah, yall both stupid," follows Chima.

"Naw aint nobody retarded I just aint gonna have nobody disrespecting my Mama house," says Roddy.

"Nigga why the fuck would I disrespect your Mama house knowing I gotta sleep there every night," Ricci jokes.

Everyone laughs. "Fuck you. I aint in the mood. Your ass was about to get beat the hell up," says Roddy. "Yo did you get that smoke? I'm ready to blow some steam off right quick," he says looking over to Bobby.

"Nigga you don't smell this shit?" asks Bobby as he pulls out a dub sack of weed. "He said this was some Afghani Kush."

"Oooh let me see that shit," Chima says as he reaches his hand out as Bobby passes him the smoke. "Damn this shit pretty as hell," says Chima as he admires the sticky, purplish weed.

"Fuck all that pretty shit. Let's smoke that shit, I told you I'm ready to get high. Plus we need to get from in front of my crib," Roddy says.

"Alright cool. We can go to Deshauna's house, her Mama don't give a fuck if we smoke in there," says Bobby.

"Damn right lets go," says CHima. "I'm tryna fuck her little sister Tiara. I think she like me."

"Nigga don't nobody like your little big headed ass," says Roddy.

"Fuck you. You just mad cause I'm only 14 and I get more bitches then yo wide nose ass."

"Nigga you crazy," says Roddy.

"I think he gotta point," says Ricci.

"Fuck you too nigga," spats Roddy. "Your ass aint got no bitches. All you got is Deja and the only reason she fuck with you is cause she can walk all over your gullible ass."

"Hell naw nigga. You know I run shit."

"What? Nigga I saw you tying her shoe the other day," says Roddy.

Everyone laughs. "Fuck you," says Ricci. "Matter fact I don't give a fuck. At least I get some pussy. I know your hand tired by now. Yo ass gon end up the 40 year virgin."

All three boys laugh at Roddy's expense. "Fuck all yall. Fuck is we still sitting here for anyway?" says Roddy.

"My bad," says Bobby. "I was too busy enjoying the show," he says as he cranks up the car and turns on the music full blast.

They travel singing along to 21 Savage and Gucci Mane. Looking at them you'd think they were shooting a music videos as they act out every lyric of the songs. Like always the music makes them forget about any petty disagreements they were having. When it was all said and done they loved each other, they might fuss and fight but guaranteed if an outsider tried to do the same they'd most likely go to war and die for one another.

"Oh, Shit," says Bobby, as he discretely turns down the radio.

"What?" Roddy asks as he looks back. "Aw man, it's the fucking police. Fuck. Fuck. Fuck," he says panicking.

"Chill bro? Stop looking back," Bobby says as he attempts to remain calm. "Just chill."

"Fuck," screams Chima.

"It's cool. It's cool. I told you I changed the license plates."

Bobby was right. He had indeed changed the license plate. He'd took them off of his Mothers old Station Wagon that was parked in their back yard. They hadn't drove it in months due to the fact that it needed a new transmission.

This plan would have been perfect had he not forgotten one small fact. The plates were expired. Big mistake. Even if 'Constipated Arieus' wasn't the cop behind them there was still a pretty good chance that they'd be pulled over. Think about it. Four black teens in fancy car blasting gangster rap. Need I say more?

Within seconds everyone in the car's worse nightmare ensued. Arieus smiles as he turns on the sirens, causing everyone's heart to drop to the pit of their stomach.

"Oh shit," they yell as the light turns green.

"Fuck that. I'm outta here," says Bobby as he steps on the gas.

"Yeah, let's get outta here," says Chima.

"Oh my God," follows Roddy as he prays to himself.

"Go, Go, Go," says Ricci as Bobby speeds his way through traffic as Arieus tails behind.

Bobby is focused. In all honesty he'd sort of dreamed of a day like this. Driving was his thing. Even growing up, he never played with action figures, only cars. And as he grew older and all the kids feigned over playing Madden and Mortal Combat, he instead preferred games such as Need for Speed and Grand Turismo. His love for cars was unquestionable.

Don't think for a second this was his first rodeo when it came to stealing vehicles. No, this was his passion. Being poor and unable to afford a car of his own, he'd been taking his parents whip while they were asleep since about 13. Shortly after that, his late brother Kody taught him how to hot wire vehicles and it was a wrap.

Well sort of. The year was 2015 Most of the cars he liked weren't really hot wireable anymore. So instead, he'd found more creative ways to get the cars he desired. Some days he'd steal the keys from teachers, taking their vehicles on joy rides during the school day and returning the car before dismissal. Other times he'd trade dope for junkies cars. It might sound crazy but there are a lot of functioning addicts walking around who'd give their soul for a hit and Bobby took full advantage.

Another one of his schemes on getting cars was to find a way to sneak off with a girlfriend or friends parents keys and go make a spare. Then the next night while they were asleep he'd have full reign to do whatever he desired. They'd wake up in the morning fussing at their kids blaming them for the fact that their car smelled of weed, alcohol and sex,

However, this particular car came a little easier. After being invited to the crib of a girl whose parents were set to go out of town for the night, they suddenly returned. Thinking fast, Bobby quickly hopped out the second floor window. Only now he was stranded.

With no phone nor way of getting home he had no choice but to walk. Luckily as he strolled, he came across a man leaving his candy red Camaro unattended, still running as he trotted into his house. Unbelieving of what he'd witnessed. He scoped out he scene for a while before finally building up enough courage to run over and hop in.

After pulling off and heading down the street undetected, in his head he was sure this was a gift from above.

Later that night he switched the tags with the ones in his back yard and parked the whip a few blocks down from his house. And all of that led to where we are in the story right now.

Ok, so keep in mind this car was a Camaro. It wasn't just some every day old Toyota. It was fast. Bobby had already tested it out on the interstate the night before so he knew how much it could get up. Still, this was the real test. This was live action. Every skill he'd acquired over the years would now be needed. So far he was doing magnificent. Maneuvering in and out of traffic, swerving from lane to lane, speeding through red lights, making it an almost impossible task for Arieus to keep up. Ultimately forcing him to call for back up.

"Yo where we going?" asks Ricci frantically.

"Nigga I don't fucking know," shouts Bobby as he nearly wrecks into an oncoming car.

"Oh shit," everyone screams as their life's flash before their eyes.

"I got it, I got it," shouts. Bobby. "Chill. Chill," he says remaining calm, eyes locked on the road ahead of him.

"Stop the car," pleads Roddy as he looks back fearfully. "Just stop the car bro," he whines.

"Hell naw I can lose these niggas," says Bobby as he continues to speed away.

"Oh shit," everyone yells as Bobby runs through a busy intersections. "AHHHH," they all screams as they sped toward a blue ford focus.

No matter how well Bobby's skills were there was no escaping the crews unfortunate fate. BOOOM! The cars collide as each boy jerks in their seatbelts. Thank God he'd stepped on the break right in the knick of time, allowing both cars to only cause minimal damage. Still, like a chain reaction, the vehicles behind them were forced to step on the breaks as well. Only they weren't nearly as blessed as the boys.

"Yall good?" asked Bobby, looking around to his friends.

"Yeah," they all say as they feel over their bodies frantically.

"Let's get the fuck out of here," shouts Bobby, as all four doors swing open at once.

They hop out the car jetting down the street with only one thing on their mind; getting away.

"Fuck," screams Arieus, slamming his fist onto his air bag as he watches the boys skate away freely.

Looking back at Arieus's vehicle's hood in the air, smoke rising from the engine, Bobby feels victorious. Always the risk taker he screams"Fuck the Police," as he darts through traffic, briefly making eye contact with Arieus.

"Oh I see right now what time it was. That little nigga who was driving was the kid you smoked. Your ass had a damn vendetta against him. You felt like he took some of your control away. Yep, I see exactly how it played out now," says Pete, laying back nodding his head.

"Well. Maybe you're right," replies Arieus in his usual position.

"Man it aint no damn maybe. You don't even have to tell me no more of the story. You felt like you lost so you had to do whatever it took to win. Man that shit is fucked up."

"Yeah maybe it was."

"Man you keep saying this maybe stuff. Aint no maybe. That shits fucked up. Bruh, that shit a real sensitive subject for me. I aint tryna judge you or nothing. I can see that life bought you to that point. It's just that shits personal to me."

"How so?"

"Nigga yall the fuckin police. Yall got the power to change a person's whole life. But a lot of yall motherfuckers choose to be negative and do whatever yall can to make sure you fuck us up. What happened to yall being here to protect and to serve? Seem like all yall out there worried about getting revenge and shit. It's like I wish there was a way they could know who the fuck they was hiring before they put yall out on the street. Yall see a little nigga out there committing crimes and shit and the first thing yall think about is locking them up or even worse killing them. What about kicking them some knowlege? You never thought of that? You could be the one who could help change the world if you just stayed positive and tried to help."

"No," Arieus quickly states. "I don't live in a fantasy word. I live in the real world. Its dog eat dog. I don't give a fuck if I'm the police or not. Nobody gives a fuck about me so why should I give a fuck about anyone else. What am I supposed to do? Help every little delinquent out. It's a fucking waste of time. I'm not gonna put all my effort into helping a motherfuckrer out for him to just go back to doing the same damn thing. Fuck that. I'm gonna do whatever it takes to make my life easier. Fuck everybody."

"Man we just can agree to disagree. I got life in prison and I still believe its good people out there."

"Suit yourself."

"I will. I have no other choice. I'll drive myself crazy if I think everyone is bad. Fuck that I got faith."

"Ok Mr. Faith man. Is it alright if I go on with my story? As you can see it's almost over."

"Sure go right ahead," Pete replies, shaking his head once again.

2015

Cloudy day, it's not raining but the sky is dark and gloomy. It appears as if the sun may be off taking a nap. No birds are chirping, nothing. It's ugly, just like Arieus's attitude as he and Ed cruise in an awkward silence.

"You're not still thinking about that kid are you?" asks Ed.

"No. Not really," replies Arieus, casually.

He's lieing, in reality he couldn't get Bobby off of his brain since the incident had happened 8 day's prior. He felt disrespected and had even had one of his pissy nightmares where Bobby and his friends were trying to kill him the night before. He didn't know how or when he'd seek revenge but he knew he would. He just had to be patient.

"Ay man what's up, why you so quiet? We've been working together for three months and I don't know anything about you."

"Why do you need to know anything about me?" asks Arieus, never taking his eyes off of the road

"I mean we work together every day and I don't even know if you're married. Gotta girl, where you grew up, where you live, Got any kids. I don't know anything man."

209

Before speaking, Arieus looks over to Ed, confused. "Why do you need to know where I live? In fact why do you need to know anything about me?"

"I don't really needa know where you live," replies Ed. "But I'm just saying I do wanna know who I'm working with."

"You're working with Arieus Hatch."

"You know what I mean. It's just that I'd like to get to know you a little better."

"Sounds pretty gay to me."

"Naw man," Ed chuckles. "Nothing like that. I'm just saying, maybe we got some of the same interests or something. Maybe we can talk sometimes instead of riding though the city not saying anything to one another."

"I never told you that you couldn't talk," replies Arieus still never taking his eyes off of the road.

"Well fuck it. I'll tell you a little about myself. Let's see. Where do I start. Ok, I've been married for about two years now. We got a little boy, Jason. I love him," Ed says as he smiles at the mere thought of his son. "My wife wants a girl. I guess I sort of do too." Ed says, appearing to be thinking. "Ok. I'm from Virginia Beach, born and raised. My Dad and Uncles are all cops. Been wanting to be one my whole life. I always just wanted to know that I'm making a difference in this world. It makes me feel like I have a purpose," he said. "I just always wanted to help make the world a better place for my kids in the future. Ya know, just really leave my mark on this place before I go."

"Better place," Arieus says, sarcastically. "Good luck."

"Huh?"

"This world aint shit. Every time you lock a criminal up two more are born."

"Wow. Is that how you really think?" he asks, looking over to Arieus. "So let me ask you this, what exactly are you in it for?"

"The power. The control."

"Seriously?" Ed asks.

"Seriously," Arieus replies, staring over to Ed, emotionless.

Suddenly a message comes across their Laptop screen that reads 'HOMICIDE ON BEACHVIEW AVE'.

"First job of the day," says Ed, happy to change the subject.

They quickly arrive to a street filled with ambulamses, squad cars and detectives.

"Man it's a friggin circus out here," says Ed. "Wonder what the hell is going on."

Disregarding him Arieus parks in an open spot alongside the curb. Slowly stepping out he takes a deep breath before moving forward. Looking around it seems as if all eyes focused on him. Ignoring the stares he marches towards the apartment building where a woman is being pushed out of the front door on a stretcher.

Pokerfaced, he continues to walk. Heart pounding a 100 miles per minute, he is unsure of just how to feel or react. Something tells him that the woman on the stretcher is his mother, Jalisa. He'd known for some time now that she lived in the apartment complex. With the thought that it could be her, he'd attempted to brace himself the entire drive over but upon seeing her being wheeled out, he realized that there may be no correct way to plan out how to witness something of the sort.

Still, not %100 percent sure it was her, he hoped that his thoughts were wrong and loathed not being in control of himself once again because of his family. No matter how much he tried to remove himself from them, they still somehow always kept a hold on him.

"No," screamed Amanda as she rushed out of the front door. "Not my Mama."

That was all the confirmation he needed. Not long after, Faith and Grace who were now grown women silently sobbed, consoling one another as they trotted out of the same door.

Right behind them walked Cameron, he's a teen by now and clearly the strongest of the bunch. He somberly strolled by himself.

Tears fall, yet he still manages to keep himself calm, unwanting of comfort he yells, "Get off of me! Get the fuck off of me," as an officer attempts to wrap his arm around his shoulder.

Still locked in on his destination, Arieus heads over to the stretcher as his superior, Lieutenant Dan spots him and walks towards his direction.

"How you doing Arieus?" asks Lieutenant Dan.

Staring straight ahead, Arieus fails to acknowledge him.

Confused, Ed follows behind oblivious to what is going on. He's never seen Arieus Ignore Dan before. "What's up with him?" Ed asks.

"That's his mother," says Dan as he and Ed watch Arieus from behind.

Finally he arrives at the stretcher before they are set to cart her into the ambulance. Breathing heavily, he wants a close up. After everything that went on growing up he still had an uncontrollable desire to see his Mother for himself.

As he stepped closer, his family grew enraged. "Fuck your black ass doing here….Motherfucker… You aint part of this fucking family," screams Amanda, voice raspy from years of ciggarete's.

"Yeah, we don't need you here." follows Grace.

"Fuck you been at? You don't care about us. And we don't care about your Uncle Tom ass," adds Cameron as they circle around him.

"You making all this money and not one time have you tried to help her," yells Faith.

As if he and Jalisa were the only people around, Arieus mentally blocks out his estranged siblings, pulling back the sheet over his Mothers, still, lifeless face.

After not seeing her up close in years, he knew this would be the last time he'd ever view her and for the first time in God knows how long, emotions grew heavy and a tear sprouted from his eye lids.

"Damn Mom Dukes died? That's tough. What happened?" asks Pete, still laying back?

"Some guy she was dating shot her three times in the stomach. I heard after she got out of jail everything just went downhill. Couldn't get her life together."

"What do you mean you heard? You never went back to see her?"

"Yeah, sort of. I never actually talked to her or anything but I drove by a lot. Saw her sitting outside smoking and stuff. She looked pretty bad."

"So you mean to tell me you rode past and saw your mother looking bad and it never made you want to stop and speak?"

"No."

"Damn. Well then what the hell do you mean you heard things had really went downhill? How the hell did you hear it if you never stopped to speak?"

"I mean I still lived in the city. To most of my family members who'd seen me grow up I was the one who made it. Yeah, they hated Policeman but they still looked at me as a success.

Especially compared to my siblings. My sisters were all on section 8, living from check to check and my brother was in and out of Police custody. Every time I'd bump into someone from Tim's family they'd always run down all the new gossip. It's like they were happy to see my family doing bad without Tim."

"So how that shit make you feel when they told you how they was doing? It didn't' make you wanna help?"

"Fuck no. I loved the fact that the one they all treated like an outcast was actually doing better than them all. To tell the truth, I sometimes smiled as I rode past my Mom. Seeing her with wrinkles all over her face and old nasty ass clothes."

"Damn bro. That's your Mom though. Your Mom," he repeats. To tell the truth you never really said too many things that she did bad to you."

"Are you crazy? She let all that shit go down. She watched me get tortured," says Arieus, strongly. "She had the power to change all that. Or at least try, and she did nothing."

"Damn. So how you feel when your sibling was mad at you though? Saying all that shit about not helping and shit. That aint make you feel bad?"

"Can't lie. It kinda did. I don't know why. It was something I couldn't control. It did make me question myself."

"Well shit at least you know you're human. Think that's why you cried?"

"Nope. The feeling of questioning my actions only lasted for a second. As they kept throwing jabs at me it sort of started to bring back old memories of my childhood. It kinda made me feel unwanted again."

"Ok. So let me ask you this. Since you know that killing Tim altered their life. It aint make you feel sad that you were part of the reason they turned out the way they did?" asked Arieus.

"I can't lie, like I said, I did question some things," Arieus says before pausing for a brief second. "I'm going to tell you some real shit man. No matter who you are. How tough you are or what your Mom has done to you. Seeing her laid out dead is a feeling I can't explain. Shit hurts. But deep down I just had to realize it wasn't my fault. I only did what I had to do. It's a cold world."

"I'm pretty sure I already know the answer to this. But did you by any chance go to the funeral? Or was that pretty much out of the question."

"You guessed it. It was definitely out of the question. I had no Dad and my Mom was dead. I went home that night and deleted her and my family out of my memory. I had always been alone anyway. It was nothing new."

"So you just went on with everyday life?"

"That's exactly what I did. Back to business as usual."

2015

Derrell Wallace, a young upbeat Black man in his early 20's walks down the sidewalk along with his 16 year old sister, Tammy Wallace. They don't usually spend too much time together but today was different.

Earlier, Derrell had been standing, kicking it on the corner when a group of his friends noticed his sister walking down the street. Like most young men their age, they had a few choice words to say about her curvy figure. Growing angry, instead of beating every one of their asses like he would have done in past instances, Derrell instead takes the grown up approach. Removing himself from the situation, he decides to walk his sister home. On the way he makes sure he schools her on the slick ways of the niggas she's soon to come across in the world.

"Yo. You needa stop wearing all that tight ass shit," Derrell says as he looks down at Tammy's outfit.

"This aint even tight," she replies.

Too be honest, it was. It wasn't like she was out looking like a whore or anything. Still, the dress she sported sure didn't leave too much for the imagination. If you stared hard enough you could even see the pattern of her underwear.

"What?" Derrell, exclaims. "If it get any tighter it'd be painted on."

"Whatever. Mommy bought it."

"I'ma have to have a lil talk with her. Yall getting outta control," Derrell says, shaking his head as Tammy chuckles. This wasn't anything new. Derrell, had always been an overprotective brother. In a way she sort of liked it. Since their Father had went away to prison he was one of the only males figures she had. "Got all my homeboys outside looking at you like you a piece of meat. Yall must won't me to go back to jail," Derrell added.

"I hope it was Quan who was looking at me," she says laughing.

"Girl you bouta make me beat your ass," he says playfully raising his hand at her.

Shortly after, the two sibling take a look back. They notice that there is a police unit slowly riding towards them. It's Ed and Arieus, Arieus in the driver's seat. Being that they were'nt doing anything wrong, Derrell and Tammy ignore them, resuming their conversation.

This doesn't sit too well with Arieus. He hates when he doesn't get the fear he feels he so rightfully deserves. As a result he stops the car a few feet in front of the two.

"Man what the hell do they want?" asks Derrell looking over.

"I don't know," Tammy says as they approach the car.

"Pull your pants up," says Arieus to Derrell as they walk by.

"Pull my pants up for what? I'ma grown ass man," Derrell snaps back.

"What did you say boy? I said pull your pants up," Arieus shouts out the window.

"Come on bro. Why you fucking with me? Its people out here robbing and raping and you worried about my pants," says Derrell, looking back, still never stopping.

"Bro?" asks Arieus, seeming to be offended.

"Derrell just pull your pants up," says Tammy.

"Hell naw," Derrell snaps. "It aint no law that says my pants gotta be pulled up. He fucking with me for no reason. What he gonna do? Arrest me?" Derrell asks.

"Do what your little fast girlfriend says and pull up those pants," barks Arieus.

Knowing that he was only trying to get under his skin Derrell ignores him. Surely this infuriates Arieus, feeling even more disrespected he throws the car in park, hops out cuffs in hand, storming over to them as both Tammy and Derrell's eyes widen.

"Come here," Arieus says as he grabs at Derrells wrists.

221

"Yo. What the fuck you doing? Yo get this nigga," Derrell pleads to Ed who'd just stepped outside the police cruiser. Unsure of just how to handle the situation, he stands, staring blankly.

"You have the right to remain silent. Anything, you say--," says Arieus.

"Yo," shouts Derrell as he resists, pulling his arm away from Arieus's grip.

"I'm going to get Mommy," screams Tammy as she races down the street, while Arieus and Derrell continue to wrestle.

In no time she arrives home, bursting through the door. Her mother Cynthia Lewis, a middle aged heavy set woman lays across the couch watching television.

"Girl, why you barging in my house like that?" barks Cynthia.

"Ma its Derrell. The police, they got him," she says running out of breath.

"Got Derrell? Where?" replies, Cynthia, quickly hopping up.

"Down the street," says Tammy. "Come on you gotta help."

Not wasting a second they both jet out of the front door.

After a while, Derrell finally gives in, allowing Arieus to gain control, slamming him to the hood of his squad car as Ed tries to contain the small crowd of Derrell supporters who had now gathered.

"Got ya," Arieus says as he slaps the cuffs onto Derrell. "What the fuck you got in there?" he questions as he drops his hand into his front pockets.

"Fuck off me. I already told your ass I aint got shit," Derrell yells.

By now Cynthia and Tammy have finally made it back. "My baby," Cynthia screams as she rushes towards Derrell.

"It's ok Mama," says Derrell, looking over to her.

"Hold on, ma'am," Arieus shouts, still holding on to Derrell.

"That's my son," she replies still moving forward.

"Back up lady," shouts Arieus. "He's been arrested for disorderly conduct."

"Disorderly Conduct?" Derrells screams. "I aint even do shit. You came out here bothering me."

"Yeah Ma. He aint even do nothing," says Tammy.

"Well he can tell that to the judge," says Arieus as he begins to drag Derrell towards his backseat.

"I told you they be fucking with me," replies Derrell, turning to look at Cynthia as he walked.

He wasn't lying, even though he had been known to get into his fair share of trouble over the years, just for the simple fact that Police never thought he received the time he deserved for his crimes, they always treated him like a criminal no matter what the case.

Not that, that anything to do with the way Arieus was treating him. Before that day, he had no prior knowledge of who the hell Derrell was, he was just treating him like he treated everybody; like shit.

"Man this some bullshit," says a Bystander.

"Motherfucking pigs always coming out here starting trouble. I bet they won't go to them white folk neighborhood and try that shit," says another, angrily.

"Calm down. Calm down," says Ed as the crowd grows larger.

"It's ok Ma. I'ma be right out. We gon sue these motherfuckers," says Derrell as Arieus stuffs him into the back seat.

"Hell yeah," shouts another bystander, causing the crowd to become antsy.

"Why you push him in like that?" asks Cynthia, rushing over to the car.

"Shut the hell up," demands Arieus as he looks back.

224

The crowd grows rowdy. "Yo don't talk to her like that," says a man.

"Show some fucking respect. That's a lady," says another.

"He don't care," says one lady.

"Ya damn right I don't. You ready Ed?" Arieus asks after slamming the back door, looking back at the spreading crowd.

"Why you gotta take him to jail?" asks Cynthia.

"Didn't I tell you to shut up lady," Arieus asks, pointing to Cynthia, sternly.

"Don't be talking to my Mama like that," screams Tammy.

"The both of you better shut up before you join his ass," Arieus blurts back.

"I don't know who he thinks he is," says Cynthia looking around." I'm gonna get his badge number," she says before storming towards the driver side door, where Arieus is attempting to sit down. "Excuse me," Cynthia says before tapping Arieus's shoulder.

Acting as if he hadn't seen her coming, Arieus quickly turns around, mase in hand, spraying her inches away from her eyes.

She screams as Derrell shouts, "What the fuck. Leave my Mama alone," while banging his head onto the glass window.

"Mama," screams Tammy as she and the rest of the crowd rush over to her defense.

"Get Back," says Arieus, backing away, holding the mase in the air, threatening to spray more as he called back-up into his walky talky.

"Aw shit," says Ed. He rushes in to his partners aide as the crowd becomes angrier. Mayhem ensues as Ed is spit on causing him to pull out his tazer, shocking the man as he screams in pain.

At the same time Arieus sprays mase and tazes into the crowd like a mad man. Looking at him, it wasn't at all hard to realize that he was enjoying every second of this. A bright, evil grin sat plastered on his face as his eyes twinkled in excitement.

Not Ed though, he stood ten toes down, petrified, as he too called for backup as the crowd continued their loud verbal assault.

When things were said and done, along with Derrell, six other young black men had been arrested and Cynthia was forced to be rushed to the hospital, suffering from an asthma attack. If you think Arieus gave a damn. You better think again.

Later on Arieus and Ed stand in front of their personal lockers inside the Police Precinct. No different than your average high school locker room the smell of male sweat filled the small quarters as Arieus and Ed changed silently into their civilians clothes.

226

John Michael, a 30 something year old out of shape white officer walks over in nothing but a towel, throwing his attention onto the two men.

"Heard you guys had a little problem in Park Place today," says John as he opens up his locker.

"Yeah man things got a little outta hand," follows Ed as he places his right leg into his jeans.

"Fucking ignorant bums. I hate that neighborhood," John Angrily says as he undresses.

"Hey Hatch," John says looking over to Arieus. .

"Yeah," says Arieus, who had just thrown on a tightly fitted black V-neck, showcasing all of the many cuts in his upper body.

"We arrested the little thug you guys got in the accident over last week. Sixteen years fucking old."

Arieus looks over as Ed speaks. "Really?"

"Yep. Him and his little crew got caught tryna run out of Norstrom's with a bunch of designer clothes. We caught them and bought their little ass down here. Finger printed them and what do you know. Every last one of those little bastards matched up perfectly."

"That's what I'm talking about. Let them sit in Juvie for a while. That'll teach em," says Ed, buttoning up his shirt.

"Juvies packed, their only locking the serious criminal up right now. Their releasing them till their court date. Besides the driver, everyone already went home. That little fuckers still waiting for his Mom to pick him up."

"Serious criminals? Their responsible for a five car pile-up sending three people to the hospital," replies Ed, sitting down to tie his shoes.

"Yeah, I understand but hey I don't make the rules. At least we know that he's gotta show his face in court. It's better than nothing," John says as all three men stand completely dressed.

"Yeah, guess you're right," says Ed, closing his locker.

"Sad. I'll catch you guys tomorrow. I'm outta here," says John, as he and Arieus close their lockers as well before walking in the opposite direction.

"Alright man," says Ed.

"Alright John," follows Arieus.

"Alright guys."

Together Arieus and Ed strut out of the front door into the parking lot. As they walk Arieus spots Bobby and Shenita Johnson, his young mother walking ahead of them towards their vehicle. Disappointment is written all over her face as she points her index finger towards him, letting him know just how tired she was of his shit. There wasn't a week that went by when he hadn't' gotten himself into something. She, along with his Step Dad had tried everything from ass whippings, punishments, to even going out to talk about his problems over ice cream, still nothing worked.

Truth was, there wasn't probably anything anyone could do for him. At least not at the present time. He was more of the have to learn it the hard way type. Throughout his Mothers tirade, for the most part he looks as if he's lost in his own world, gazing straight ahead. Until suddenly it's as if he could feel eyes on the back of his head, he looks back and for the second time, he and Arieus make eye contact.

"That's your man right there isn't?" asks Ed.

"It sure is," Arieus says as he and Bobby continue their stare off.

"Aw man. I forgot my wife dropped me off this morning," he says looking out onto the parking lot. "My car wouldn't start. You think I could get a lift home?" asks Ed.

"Sure. Ok," replies Arieus as he finally takes his eyes from Bobby.

"Thanks man."

They hop into Arieus's black Nissan Altima, where Ed gives him the address to put into his vehicle's GPS.

"Ay Hatch," says Ed looking over to Arieus after driving for about 20 minutes.

"Whatsup?" replies Arieus, eyes still on the road.

"You think all that was necessary today?"

"What do you mean?"

"I mean I hate seeing a man's ass as I'm driving down the street too but you don't think you reacted a little--," he says as he searches for the right words. "Over the top. I mean a fucking riot started over someone sagging their pants."

Arieus sits silent for a brief second before speaking, "A riot didn't start because someone sagged their pants," he says finally looking over to Ed. "A riot started because of disrespect to a law enforcement officer."

"Yeah but don't you think you were a little disrespectful to them?"

"I got the power. They do what I say. I'm not paid to show respect. I'm paid to enforce laws and that's exactly what I did," he says before looking back at the road.

"You mind if I ask you something Arieus?"

"Sure."

"Do you get enjoyment from putting people in jail?"

"Yes," says Arieus, nodding his head. "Yes I actually do," cracking a smile.

"But their gonna be right back on the streets one day without having learned a thing."

"That's not my problem. Like I said. My job is to enforce the law. Their criminals. Their job is to break it. It's not my fault I'm better at my job then they are there's."

"Again I can't say I agree. But I have to admit I've never heard it from that point of view before."

"You have arrived at your destination," says the GPS from the Arieus's car speaker. They'd finally made it to Ed's small one story home. He dwelled in a relatively nice neighborhood. Middle class, the type where everyone's yard was neatly decorated with precisely cut grass.

"Here's my castle," Ed says. "What do ya think?"

"I think it's a home," replies Arieus.

Ed laughs. "How did I know you would say something like that? I'm just happy for it. Renting, spending money every month for something you don't own, just gets under my skin. To finally have something I can call mine, makes me feel proud."

"Cool," replies Arieus, unmoved.

"Well I'll see ya tomorrow night," says Ed as he opens the door to exit. "Sucks that we gotta do graveyard shift. But hey, somebody's gotta do it," he says as Arieus nods. "Alright man. Thanks for the ride. Appreciate it," he follows, closing the car door behind him.

Arieus nods once again, staring at the home as Ed walks in.

"Boy you crazy as hell I heard about that riot. My peoples was out there. You abused your power like a motherfucker," Pete says.

"I don't think so. When you see my uniform you can either respect it or pay the price. Simple as that."

"Yeah I guess," says Pete. "Ok, so tell me this. Exactly, how do yall niggas feel when you got that power? I kinda always wanted to know that shit."

"Strapping on that uniform I felt invinisible."

"Like a super hero or something?"

"No. Far better than that. I felt just like I felt when I had Amanda's dolls. I felt like God. I told you, control was my thing. With that badge and uniform I had control over everything. It's a feeling that can't be touched. No drug, no alcohol, nothing can compare.

"Control. Control. Control. That's all you ever talk about."

"That's all that was important to me. What can I say?"

"I gotta be honest with you man. The more you talk about that control shit, the more I do see where you coming from. I mean just sitting in here with no control over my life, I can't help but sort of feign for it. This shit is hell man, just waking up sometimes not even being able to move, it's like I got stress weighing me down or something. Not to mention the loneliness. Yo I swear loneliness gotta be some of the most painful shit in the world."

"Tell me about it," adds Arieus.

"I mean, I aint never been shot but I swear it gotta be something like it. Real shit, sometimes it's a struggle to even live. I can't even count all the times I don thought about killing myself."

"What keeps you from doing it?" asks Arieus.

"I guess like I said before, faith. That's all I got. That and my son. It aint much that I can really teach him while I'm in here, but I at least gotta show him that you can't give up. You can't be a quitter," Pete says before pausing. "Shit is just hard man," he says as he wipes a tear away.

"You alright down there?" asks Arieus.

"Yeah, man I'm good. But yeah back to what we was just talking about. I can't lie I fuck with that nigga Ed. At least I know there was a few good cops. No offense."

"Fuck Ed. His little white ass had a fairy tale view on life. He went out there every day thinking he was making some kinda change. He aint make shit. All he did was pass the time. If anybody made a change it was me. Fear. Fear is much more powerful than anything. People make better decisions when they operate outta fear."

"You must've just thought of that now because I know your ol crazy ass wont tryna put fear in nobody heart just so that they wouldn't commit no crimes. If anything it probably just made your dick hard that anybody was scared of your crazy ass."

Arieus smiles. "You're a smart man."

Ghent is one of the most affluent neighborhoods in all of Norfolk. It's a well known fact that's where the old money dwells. All of the past slave-owners, judges, and politicians had been passing down wealth for generations.

With that in mind, yes, some of the houses may appear to be a tad bit dated but best believe the moment you step foot in one of those bad boys you'd soon forget the exterior. The insides were nothing short of remarkable, marble floors, huge flat screen T.V's, and $10,000 kitchens sets.

Residents sort of lived in a different world from the rest of Norfolk. A world where wife's don't work, babies are raised by nannies, and car doors don't lock.

The car doors not locking is where this story begins.

It's 1 a.m. and Roddy and Bobby cruise down the dark suburban streets. What are they in search of? If you're thinking cars you're right, but it's not exactly what you think. In fact they're already in a stolen car, this one was an old MPV van. They were some of the best vehicles to steal. Not only because they were still hot wireable but they were large enough to stash any stolen goods they'd come across.

Yep that's right, Roddy and Bobby were on a treasure hunt. And with so many luxury cars in Ghent being left unlocked, and residents fast asleep, they were sure to come off with something of value. It was pretty much guaranteed.

"Man this neighborhood makes me nervous," says Roddy.

"Calm down, it's gonna be worth it. Imagine what these rich motherfuckers leave laying around in these damn cars. Dumb ass crackers might even leave some money in them bitches. Who knows," states Bobby before spotting a dark parking space beneath a large tree. "Park the car right there," he says, pointing up to it.

"Alright," says Roddy before cautiously pulling over into the vacant spot. "Yo we can't take all day."

"Nigga I know. I'm a pro at this criminal shit," says Bobby as he looks around at his surroundings. "We gonna get what the fuck we can, then we gon get the fuck outta here. Come on," he says as they quietly exit the vehicle.

"Don't slam the door," whispers Roddy.

"Nigga shut the fuck up. I know," he says as they both gently close their doors. "You get that side, I'ma get this side."

"Alright. We gotta be done in 10 minutes yo. I aint tryna get caught," whispers Roddy as he creeps over to his destination.

Turns out Roddy and Bobby chose the right neighborhood on the wrong night. Why? Simple. It was Arieus and Ed's final night to work the graveyard shift and Lieutenant Dan had decided to give them a break. Like Maine and Ed, their hard work hadn't gone unnoticed and they'd been assigned to patrol Ghent because nine times outta ten, the Ghent Jurisdiction was a walk in the park.

"Ghent," says Ed admiring his surroundings. "I've always wanted to live over here. Old money. I wonder how it feels to be rich," says Ed.

Arieus stares out the window. For once he's thinking exactly what Ed is, only he still doesn't speak.

"I don't know how we're going to do it but I swear I'm going to get me a million dollar home one day too. Not sure if I'll move over here though. Probably find something a little more modern," Ed says, looking over to Arieus, hoping to spark some sort of conversation.

Of course Arieus remains silent.

A few blocks over, Bobby slowly approaches a driveway being occupied by a Mercedes Benz S550. Being a lover of cars he couldn't help but to admire it's beauty, still it wasn't exactly his taste. All factory, no fancy rims, tint, nothing. He shakes his head, thinking to himself all the additions he would've added.

Getting back to the task at hand he attempts to quietly open the door. Bingo, it fly's right open. "Jackpot," he says to himself. As he silently rummages through the leather interior, he comes across a gun hidden beneath the driver side seat. "Hell yeah," he says to himself. It was a chrome 9 millimeter, shiny as a new penny. After tucking it away into his underwear, he quietly shuts the door, looking around once more before heading to the next driveway just a few feet over, only to learn that it was locked. "Fuck."

The minutes flew by and he'd managed to find a few more unlocked vehicles but being the experienced criminal he was, he knew it was time to call it a quits and of course Roddy felt the same.

"You aint got nothing?" asks Bobby as both teens slide back into their vehicle.

"Nope I'm ready to go. I don't feel good about this shit," says Roddy before noticing an IPAD and a new IPhone in Bobby's hands. "Damn you got all of that?" he asked shockingly.

"Yep. And I got this," he says as he pulls the pistol from his waisteline.

"Oh shit," says Roddy as his eyes widened.

"Yep! I can probably get like $250 for this shit," says Bobby, staring at his new baby as Roddy uses his screwdriver as a key and starts the ignition.

"You lucky as hell," says Roddy as he pulls off.

239

"Naw nigga I aint lucky. I just know what the fuck I'm doing. You an amateur."

"Yeah, yeah whatever," says Roddy as they drive towards a two story brick house with a pair of luxury cars sitting in the driveway.

"Yo. Yo. Yo. Stop right there."

"For what?" Barks Roddy. "You got enough."

"Bro just pull over," Bobby demands. "Just let me check out those two whips. I gotta good feeling about them."

"Hell naw man I told you I already feel nervous about even being around here."

"Man, park the car it's only gonna be 15 seconds."

Taking a deep breath, Roddy reluctantly agrees. "Alright. But you better hurry up," he says hesitantly as he pulls over to an open spot in front of the house, turning off the headlights.

"Thanks my nigga," Bobby says as he hops out. Jogging over to the two whips, he cautiously looks both ways before attempting to open the first car. Its locked. "Damn," he says as he trots over to the next vehicle.

Roddy stares as Bobby attempts the second. It's open. He looks over to Roddy, throwing him a wink and a smile, before diving in.

Growing impatient Roddy says to himself, "Nigga hurry up," as he timidly looks around before spotting headlights approaching. Petrified, his initial instinct was to press down on the gas. Luckily he was better than that, he knew he couldn't leave his boy hanging. Immediately rolling down the passenger side window, he calls out to Bobby, "Ay nigga! Somebody coming down the street."

"Oh shit," says Bobby as he looks back.

As fearful sweat shot down his body, Roddy looks back once more, now discovering it was far worse than he'd thought.

Trying to be as smooth as possible, Bobby closes the door, ducking down between the two vehicles hoping they'd simply ride pass leaving him undetected.

The seconds seemed to be hours and truthfully Roddy was losing his mind. Unable to take the pressure he punches down on the gas, speeding away into the night.

"Why in the hell did they pull off like that?" asks Ed from the vehicle as they approach the house where Bobby is still crouched down.

With nowhere to run, Bobby dives beneath the vehicle. Closing his eyes, he prays. "Lord Please let me get out of this. I promise I won't do anything like this again. I'ma go to church, I'ma do what my Mama and Pops say. I'ma even clean up the bathroom and you know I hate doing that. Lord please let me be safe."

Reopening his eyes he discovers Arieus and Ed cruising by slowly in front of the house. Realizing it would be damn near impossible for the two to spot him, he figured he was safe. That was until Arieus shined his flash light into the driveway. At that moment, the two make eye contact once again. "Fuck," Bobby screams before, rolling out from beneath the car, taking off into the night.

"It's the kid," says Ed, spotting Bobby as he made his great escape.

"Get him," shouts Arieus, never for once taking his eyes off of his target.

Reversing the vehicle, Ed travels on hot pursuit. "We gotta suspect on foot," he says into his walky talky.

"Get his ass," Arieus urges Ed once again as they pull into a cul de sac where Bobby is running for dear life in the middle of the street.

Going with his instincts Bobby darts into the back yard of a nearby house.

"Stop the car," Arieus shouts. "Stop the car," he screams after Ed failed to move fast enough.

Coming to a screeching halt Ed stops the vehicle as Arieus wasted no time bolting out of the vehicle.

As it turns out, the backyard Bobby had chosen led to a huge man made lake. As branches and leaves smacked him across the face he searches in desperation for an open path, knowing the officers weren't far behind.

Simultaneously Ed Parks the car, joining his partner in search of their suspect.

At this time Arieus had finally made it to the backyard.

Still searching for a way out, Bobby trips over a rock falling to the ground. "Fuck," he screams. Looking back he sees Arieus catching up. "Shit," he says before hopping back to his feet to continue his trail. He searched and searched, still there was nowhere to go. There was no telling what lay in the dark lake. With no exit in site and Arieus gaining on him, he decides to simply throw in the towel, turning around hands in the air. "I give up," he screams as he and Arieus face off for the final time.

"Motherfucker," shouts Arieus pointing his pistol straight ahead as Bobby's eyes bulge out of their sockets and his life flashed before he eyes.

"Oh shit," Bobby yelled as Arieus let the clip off into his adolescent chest.

"Arieus what the fuck," screamed Ed from behind as Bobby's body collided with the earth. "What the fuck," shouted Ed, finally catching up, racing to their suspect as Arieus stood, feet cemented. "You fucking killed him," he shouted.

Lowering his pistol, never speaking, Arieus walks over to Bobby's body.

"He had his hands up," says Ed as he drops to the ground next to Bobby's blood soaked frame. His chest filled with smoking holes, eyes wide open. "You killed em," Ed yelled as he checked Bobby's pulse. " He's fucking dead. He's fucking Dead man," Ed shouts, as saliva oozes out of his mouth and tears drip from his eye sockets. "You killed him man." Emotionless Arieus leans down to check for himself as Ed continued to scream. "You fucking killed him! He gave up man. He fucking gave up."

After patting down Bobby's blood-drenched soulless body, Arieus looks up with a smirk. "He tried to kill me," he said, as he pulled the stolen gun from Bobby's waistline.

Ed stares into the eyes of Arieus and Bobby's. There was no difference.

Later in the night yellow tape is wrapped around Bobby's murder scene as newscasters and Policeman invade the once quiet neighborhood.

Bobby's mother Shenita shouts in agony as her husband Lew Johnson, attempts to be strong, comforting her as his bloodshot eyes look to the sky in search for answers.

244

"They killed my baby. They killed my baby," shouts Shenita as she breaks away from Lew, jumping up and down unsure of what to do with herself. "They killed my baby."

Like a bubble, Lew's emotions soon burst, spiraling him out of control, leaving him swinging erratically in the air, as tears fall from his eyes. Dropping to his knees he beats the concrete with his bare hands.

While only a few feet away, Jack Ramsey the local new casters holds a microphone to, 'Deborah Cross' the older sister of Bobby's Mother. She stares into the camera, visibly hurt, before speaking.

"It's just sad. My sister and Brother in law just lost their oldest son 6 months ago because of a crazy drunk driver. Now this. You know it's really really sad," she continues, shaking her head from right to left, peering deeply into the camera "I mean Bobby was such a nice kid. Yeah I know he's been getting into trouble lately. But I think he's just been acting out because of the loss of his brother. They were extremely close. But as far as these officers accusations that he attempted to shoot them. That is a lie. A bold face lie. I've known that boy since the day he was born. He'd never do a dumb thing like that. Those punk ass officers just took someone's child. Someone's grandson. Someone's friend. He could've grown up to be the president of the United States. The truth will come out sooner or later. You can bet your last dollar on that," she says pointing into the camera. "They will pay. They will pay," she repeats before bursting into tears. "Get that damn camera out of my face," she says before rushing over to join her sister and brother in law.

A little further down the street Bobby's killer Arieus, along with Ed and Lieutenant Dan stand talking amongst themselves. Arieus and Dan remain calm while Ed on the other hand shakes uncontrollably, fighting back tears as his body rocks from right to left.

"Alright guys, you know you have to go on a leave of absences until we finish investigating. Don't worry you guys did the right thing. I had to kill once myself. It comes with the job. Hey, better him than you. The kid had a gun," he says as he speaks with his hands. "You did the right thing. It's not like you just woke up this morning and said you're gonna kill a guy. You were scared. What other choice did you have? Just go home and get some rest. Try not to let things beat you up. You're lucky to have a partner who's so quick on his feet," he says directing his words to Ed. "You never know if he hadn't got the first shot off that kid could've shot either one of you.

"Excuse me Lieutenant Dan," says a fellow officer a few feet away from the trio.

"I'll see you guys later. I have to go handle a few things," he says before walking away.

As he trots off Ed and Arieus compete in one of Arieus's favorite pastimes; a stare off. There was so much Ed wanted to say. The words just wouldn't seem to come out.

Finally without saying a word, he storms off into the night.

"Damn so that's it? That shit should have been a movie," Pete says standing excitedly to his feet. "Yo you need to write a book or something. That shit was popping. I aint saying I agree with none of that crazy shit you did. But damn."

"Hold on. Hold on. I never told you that was it."

"What? There's more?" Pete asks.

2015

Never in a million years would Ed have ever thought that this is how life in the Police Force would be. As he sat alone in his driveway. He prayed to God for understanding. He had been placed in such an uncomfortable position. What he'd seen was wrong. On every level. The image of Arieus killing Bobby in cold blood was one that he couldn't shake. Over and over it replayed throughout his head.

In his heart he knew he should have told Lieutenant Dan from the start what had occured. But he couldn't. He didn't have it in him. Honestly, if he'd said anything he would sort of be going against the code. See, the Police are probably the biggest organized gang in history. And similar to any gang they have written and unwritten rules that must be followed.

Just like the streets, not telling on your fellow Policeman was normal protocol. Even if he was to say something, he'd be ridiculed and maybe even forced to quit. No other officer would be able to trust him. Still with knowing all of that, the thought of letting it all out never seemed to leave his mind.

It's just the way Arieus had looked at him that had him apprehensive. He stared in a way that felt demonic. It's like he had found a way inside of Ed's head and was whispering. "Say anything and you're next."

Actually the whispering hadn't quite left, every so often on his ride home, just when he was on the verge of doing what he thought was right, he'd hear Arieuss' voice again. In one instance it had shook him up so much that it had nearly caused him to swerve over to the next lane. What he witnessed was literally driving him crazy.

For hours he sat, shaking, alone in his car, searching deep inside for the strength and energy to walk into the house and after countless attempts he'd finally found enough within himself. He wasn't sure if he'd be able to make it all the way to his bedroom but at least if he fell asleep on the cold hardwood floor of his living room he'd be in the comforts of his own home. The way he saw it, just breathing in the same air as his family may have been what he needed. Certainly sitting alone wasn't helping. So, after taking one final breath, realizing it was nearly 6 in the morning, he finally steps out of the vehicle. "Lord help me," he says to himself.

Not a single second after his foot hit the pavement a bullet entered his head from the back, splattering blood and brains into the atmosphere.

It was Arieus, point blank range, dressed in all black with a hoody and skull cap over his head. As Ed's limp body plummeted to the ground, Arieus stood over him flashing a smile before tucking his weapon back into his holster. In the recent years he'd advanced his killing technique, investing in a silencer, he was able to kill Ed without so much as a peep.

While Ed laid in a pool of blood, Arieus through on his hoody, only to stroll down the street as if nothing had happened.

It's was almost four hours later before a neighbor found Ed's body.

"You killed Ed?" Pete screamed, hopping up to look over to Arieus once again.

"You gonna tell the world?" asked Arieus.

"Damn my bad," Pete whispered. "Man that's fucked up," he said back in his regular speaking voice. "I remember them talking about that shit on CNN. Kept tryna say one of Bobby's homeboy's did it or something. They even talked about getting you extra protection because they was probably gonna be coming after you next. The whole time it was your ass who did it. It's a crazy world."

"Can you blame me?"

"Hell yeah I can blame you motherfucker. You the one who did it. Who the hell else can I blame?"

"I had no choice, he was too nervous. He would snitch."

"Yeah you right. But damn. All this shit is just so new to me," says Pete before pointing over to Arieus. "You a fucking cop. I never would've thought I'd hear the things that I heard today."

"Yeah. What can I say."

"So the whole time your case was on trial did you ever think they would convict you?"

252

"Sometimes. Everybody seemed to think I did it on purpose."
Arieus says, nodding slowly.

"Nigga you did. I remember looking at the news and seeing
one of the old white neighbors in the neighborhood you killed Bobby
in say he heard Ed shouting, *'You fucking killed him'*. Soon as I heard
that I knew you had done it. Aint no white man gonna send a cop to
prison for no little black boy unless they ass was telling the truth."

"Yeah, you're right. But they couldn't prove it. Now do you
understand why I killed Ed?"

"Nigga I aint never say I didn't understand. I was just letting
you know that you aint shit. So tell me this. What was going through
your mind during the trial?"

"At the end of the day. I still am a black man. And with all the
national outcry, protests and all that Black lives Matter bullshit, I
really was just preparing myself to go to jail. They gave me paid leave
but all that did was give me more time to think."

"What was you thinking about?"

"My control being over. I knew if I landed in jail, I'd never get
the feelings that I loved ever again. I started drinking, just doing
anything to pass the time."

"Oh, so that's how you got the drunk in public charge that
landed you in here."

"Yep."

"But hold on. I remember earlier you saying how you hated the taste of alcohol."

"Still do. It's just that after trying it again years later, I grew an appreciation for the world it entered you into."

"Ok Ok, I can understand that. I'm more of a smoker myself, that shit takes all my stress away. I actually been smoking every day for the past two years."

"How so?"

"Nigga I been in prison. Not jail. Prison is basically just like the streets, anything you can get out there we can get in there, well except for the bitches."

"I never knew that."

"Well you learn something new every day. I damn sure learned some shit today from your ass. But anyway back to you. How did you feel when they sentenced you for the drunk in public charge?"

"To tell the truth I figured they'd do something like that. I guess the judge thought it would make the world feel better since I'd beat the murder charge."

"Yeah but it didn't."

"Hell no. Everybody already knew why they did it," Arieus replies.

"Ok so let me ask you this. Out of all the shit that the black media had to say about you. Did it ever make you feel bad about killing Bobby? After all the nigga was just a kid."

"Nope. I actually think I did him a favor. This world is cold. I gave him a way out. His parents should thank me."

"What?" Pete, exclaims. "Yo you a crazy dude. You might have PTSD or something. You need to get checked out."

"Hey. Maybe I do. But the way I see it, the whole world is crazy, so fuck it."

"So after this do you plan on going back into the force?"

"You better fucking believe it."

"In Norfolk?"

"I haven't' really thought about that yet," says Arieus before pausing. "Again man thanks for listening," says Arieus, sincerely. "You don't know how good I feel to get some of that stuff out of me. It's like a weight lifted off of my shoulders. Even though I'm still in this hell hole I sort of feel free."

"No problem," Pete says as he lays back onto his rack. "Yo."

"Whatsup," replies Arieus.

"I meant to ask you. You ever have any other girlfriends after Becka?"

"Fuck no."

"Damn."

"See, in relationships you can't have control of your own feelings."

"Ok Ok. So you just live your life beating your meat all damn day?"

"There are other ways to get sex."

"Prostitutes?"

"Maybe."

"You a nasty ass nigga," Pete says before laughing. "But foreal don't that shit get lonely."

"Yep. I can't say that it doesn't. But again like most things of that nature, I'm used to it."

"I wish I could, I been trying to get used to this shit for years."

Maine and Ed walk up.

"Rec time. You ready to get some fresh air Motherfucker," asked Maine.

"Hell yeah," says Pete.

"You wouldn't be coming to would you Hatch? I see you're a changed man all of a sudden," asked Eric. Arieus shakes his head as Pete slowly gets up from his rack. "Well I hope you at least plan on taking a shower later on. I don't think you've taken one since you've been here," he says as Arieus continues staring at the ceiling.

"Hurry up nigga," Maine urges Pete as he throws on his jumpsuit and sneakers. "After we take you down there, we going the fuck home. It's been a long ass day."

"Nigga shut your ass up, yall niggas aint did shit all damn week," replies Pete, as he slides his hands through the chuckhole.

They both laugh.

"You're right about something my brother," follows Eric.

Maine opens the cell to release Pete as he leads the pack down the small hallway.

"So what the hell you and that nigga been talking about?" asks Maine, as he walks directly behind Pete.

"Nothing much." says Pete, slyly smiling.

"Nothing much? Nigga yall been gossiping like two old lady's for the past 12 hours," adds Eric.

"You'll find out soon enough. The world will." says Pete still smirking.

"Huh? What the hell is that supposed to mean?" follows Maine.

"You'll see," Pete says smiling. "Ay, I need yall to do me a favor though."

"Fuck that. I'm all out of favors" says Eric. "Didn't you hear us say we're about to go home."

"I'm serious. It's important," says Pete, turning to face the two Men. "Real important."

"What is it?" asks Eric.

"It's personal. Just know I need to go down to the P.O.C. and talk to some Detectives I got some shit I gotta let them know."

"Oh shit. What the hell did that man tell you back there?" asks Maine.

"You dirty little snitch," asks Eric.

"I don't give a fuck what you say. I'm about to handle my business," Pete says with a smile.

Friday

Maine and Eric sit in the patrol room drinking coffee fiddling with their phones as a small black and white television, displays Arieus now alone staring at the ceiling in his cell.

Maine appears pleasant while Eric seems to be troubled. Neither act as if the other is in the room until Officer Long walks in.

"How you doing sir?" asks Maine, looking up with a smile.

"Sir," follows Eric, blankly.

"Hey guys. Did you here what happened after you all left last night?" asks Officer Long.

"No what happened?" asks Maine.

"I don't know if you've noticed but ol Pete's not in his cell today," he says as he points to the television screen.

"Yeah I know. We took him down to the POC last night," adds Maine.

"Boy, you guys don't know what you did," says Officer Long.

"Did we do something wrong sir?" asks Maine.

"No. No you didn't do anything. But it turns out that we may have a serial killer on our hands. Pete was able to match up about 4 other homicides besides Bobby that Arieus was responsible for, including the Officer he'd been assigned with the night of the murder."

"What?" shouts Maine. "Are you serious? I knew his ass looked a little too crazy."

"Yeah," Officer Long, says, nodding. "Pete's been with Detectives all night. Today was supposed to be his court date reguarding his appeal but I have a feeling he'll be getting out soon no matter what goes on in court. The info he gave was big. This is going to be national. They got Sheriffs on their way down to pick Arieus up right now."

"Damn. I saw them talking all day but I never knew it was that serious. Yep this is big. You hear that shit Eric," Maine says, tapping Eric on the shoulder.

Continuing to sit, Eric ignores Maine. "Excuse me," he says as he stands up, brushing past Officer Long, storming out of the room.

"What was that all about?" asks Officer Long.

"Who knows. But if I had to guess, I'd have to say it's problems with his girl again," Maine says, rolling his eyes.

A few minutes later as Eric speeds through the jail hallway he approaches Arieus cell, while a gang of Officer's trail behind him. They talk amongst themselves as they prepare to arrest Arieus.

"Motherfucker," Eric screams as he aggressively unlocked Arieus's cell, slamming it shut before flying in and dragging him from his top bunk. As he falls hard to the floor, Eric, immediately floods his face and body with blows.

"Heyyy. What the fuck," Arieus screams attempting to fight back, only it was too late.

"Ima kill you," screams Eric as he continues his rampage.

Finally the Sheriffs run up to the cell after hearing all of the commotion.

"Stop. Stop. We can handle this," says the leader as he clumsily whips out his set of keys from his pocket, only to drop them on the floor.

"No fuck that. Stand back from me," screams Eric to the Officers as he held Arieus in a choke hold between his legs with a knife to the side of his neck. "You don't know what just fucking happened to me," Eric continues.

"Just talk to us," says the Officer after picking up his set of keys while the other Officers stand back.

261

"Don't come any closer," he yells to the Officers. "Fuck talking, I'm done talking," says Eric, as drool and tears rush down his face. "You wanna know what happened to me last night? Huh? Well I'm going to tell you. I come home from work, take a shower and go to put on my shoes and you know what falls out. Huh? Huh? A fucking condom wrapper. I don't wear condoms," he yells. "So you know what that means? My girl was fucking cheating. Cheating on me," he repeats louder. "Some nigga was fucking the shit outta my bitch. In my Bed and for some reason he decides to leave me some evidence. So you know what I do? I aint say shit about it. Played it cool. But later in the night. I decided to follow her ass when she said she was going to her friend's house for a little bit. So after about 20 minutes or so we finally pull up to a house. She hops out and what do you know. It's not a fucking friend's house," Eric screams as he tightens his grip around Arieus's neck. "A fucking Cop comes to the door. The same cop who patrols my neighborhood. The same cop who I smile and wave to every day," he says before looking into each of the officers eyes who were listening to him. "She's been fucking one of you motherfuckers," he screams. "My girls been getting piped down by a cop. You motherfuckers think you can do what the fuck you want," he screams looking down to Arieus who's fighting for air. "You think you got control over the whole fucking world. Well look at you now. Look at you," he yells, looking down to Arieus, choking him harder.

"I'm sorry about what happened to you. We've all been through it. But don't make a mistake you're gonna regret. Trust me.

262

Let us handle this," the lead Officer says attempting to diffuse the situation.

"Fuck that," Eric screams. "His ass is gonna pay. He's gotta die."

"No," screams the officers before finally bursting into the cell as Eric thrust the knife into Arieus's throat....

Monday

"**AHHHHHH**," Arieus awakens, kicking and screaming.

"Yo what the fuck wrong with you," screams Pete hopping up from his rack. He, stands tall at 6'1, able to have a clear view of Arieus. Face balled up, he studies him, attempting to discover what the problem was that had interrupted his sleep. As he scanned Arieus's body who was now sitting up, he noticed what looked like urination covering Arieus's bottom half. "What the fuck," he screams before the stench hit his nose, letting him know that it was indeed urination that he smelt. "You stinky murdering bitch," screams Pete...

If you enjoyed American Maniac make sure you spread the word.

If you purchased on Amazon or Kindle please leave a review.

If you're incarcerated please request to get this book and my other novels 'American Rap Star', 'American Boy', 'Us Vs. Them', and my latest, 'American Dream', in the building!

Thank you for the support. If you need to contact me:
Phone: 757-708-4890
Facebook: Kevin Brown
Instagram: __KevinBrown
Website:KevinBrownBooks.com

Made in the USA
Middletown, DE
16 September 2022

10604013R00149